SPECIAL MESSAGE TO READERS

This book is published by
THE ULVERSCROFT FOUNDATION
a registered charity in the U.K., No. 264873

The Foundation was established in 1974 to provide funds to help towards research, diagnosis and treatment of eye diseases. Below are a few examples of contributions made by THE ULVERSCROFT FOUNDATION:

A new Children's Assessment Unit at Moorfield's Hospital, London.

•

Twin operating theatres at the Western Ophthalmic Hospital, London.

•

The Frederick Thorpe Ulverscroft Chair of Ophthalmology at the University of Leicester.

•

Eye Laser equipment to various eye hospitals.

If you would like to help further the work of the Foundation by making a donation or leaving a legacy, every contribution, no matter how small, is received with gratitude. Please write for details to:

**THE ULVERSCROFT FOUNDATION,
The Green, Bradgate Road, Anstey,
Leicester LE7 7FU. England
Telephone: (0533) 364325**

SEVEN KILLERS EAST

Stalked by vengeance-crazed desperadoes, the veteran trouble shooters defended themselves from an isolated line shack. But when the killers started burning it, their time was running out. Would this be their last showdown?

MARSHALL GROVER

SEVEN KILLERS EAST

A LARRY & STRETCH WESTERN

Complete and Unabridged

LINFORD
Leicester

First published in Australia by
Horwitz Grahame Pty Limited
Sydney

First Linford Edition
published October 1991
by arrangement with
Horwitz Grahame Pty Limited
Sydney

Copyright © 1987 by Marshall Grover
All rights reserved

British Library CIP Data

Grover, Marshall
 Seven killers east.—Large print ed.—
 Linford western library
 I. Title II. Series
 823 [F]

ISBN 0-7089-7094-X

Published by
F. A. Thorpe (Publishing) Ltd.
Anstey, Leicestershire

Set by Words & Graphics Ltd.
Anstey, Leicestershire
Printed and bound in Great Britain by
T. J. Press (Padstow) Ltd., Padstow, Cornwall

1

The Peace Seekers

"BEST damn fight since I can't remember when," enthused Milt Jacklin, boss of the J Bar ranch of Kimber County, Wyoming.

"Glad you're enjoying it," was Dr Myron Beeby's dry rejoinder. "Still a hell-raiser at heart, huh? You ought to be ashamed, you old reprobate. At your age, with a fine wife like Ula and three full-grown daughters . . ."

"Don't remind me I'm past my prime," Milt gleefully chided. "Doggone it, Doc, it makes a man feel young again — seein' them fiddlefoots beatin' the tar outa them circle Nine waddies."

"Be content to listen to this ruckus," advised the medico. "Don't try sneaking a look. You could take a flying spittoon in the face. Or a bottle. Or a chair."

Old cronies from way back, the grey-whiskered cattleman and the veteran healer had sought a neutral corner when the brawl began in the Queen of Diamonds Saloon. Mindful of their age, they had not attempted to vault the bar; they had dropped to all fours and crawled around behind it. At that, they could have chosen safer cover. Other non-combatants, however, had beaten them to the corners of the big barroom. So now they hunkered behind the bar counter while a half-dozen local cowhands made sincere and violent efforts to beat the living daylights out of two tall strangers.

"Remember now, Doc, we're their witnesses," Milt stressed. "We can't let George Hallam or his deputies throw them Texas bucks in the county jail. They didn't start it. We saw a Circle Nine man throw the first punch."

"I'm not likely to forget," said Beeby. "He missed, but the Texan didn't."

He winced and ducked. A missile, human and hefty, had hurtled clear across the bartop to crash against the rear shelves and flop beside him, out cold.

"Hot damn!" whooped Milt. "Hey, I gotta take a look-see."

"Careful," begged Beeby.

The runty J Bar boss raised just the top half of his head for a brief but appreciative appraisal of the scene of conflict. He relished what he saw, a Circle Nine man reeling from the impact of a rock-hard Texas fist, crashing against the balustrade of the staircase leading up to the private quarters of Ritchie York, the saloon's owner. Five balusters promptly lurched inward and the stair-rail sagged drunkenly. The taller Texan, a gangling six and a half footer, had his back to a side window when another cursing cowman charged him. He sidestepped nimbly and, unable to check his rush, his attacker hurtled through the window in a welter of shattering glass. Another assailant leapt onto the back of the other Texan, only to be dislodged by an elbow-jab that put him down howling, his ribs dented.

Lowering himself, Milt chuckled approvingly.

"They wouldn't have dared..." he began.

"Just a minute." Doc Beeby had found a stub of pencil and was making calculations on the back of a used envelope. "I'm doing a little figuring in advance. Let's see now..." He glanced at the still-unconscious cowhand huddled beside them. "Fractured jaw for sure, possible concussion. That'll be — well, I'll add a little to my fee. The patient's probably broke, but his boss is damn near as rich as you. What'd you see, Milt?"

"Larry Valentine hit that galoot so hard, he damn near wrecked the staircase when he went into it," grinned Milt.

"Should have to tape that one's ribs — he could've broken an arm too," opined Beeby, making another note. "What else?"

"A feller rushed Stretch Emerson and

ended up divin' through a window," recalled Milt.

"I heard the sound of breaking glass," nodded Beeby. "Uh huh. There'll be cuts, some that'll need stitching. I'll be busy till dawn I anticipate. Not much sleep for me tonight. An extra two dollars for my time I think."

"They wouldn't have dared, them Circle nine hotheads, if they knowed who them tall boys are," leered Milt. "They can't be licked! Why, if there were twice as many galoots tryin' to beat up on 'em, they'd *still* win!"

"The strangers are unbeatable?" Beeby enquired, mildly curious.

"I recognized 'em right off — didn't you?" challenged Milt.

"The names are familiar," frowned Beeby.

"Valentine and Emerson, the Texas Trouble-Shooters — and too tough to be licked." The old cattleman cocked an approving ear to the sounds of mayhem and talked on wistfully. "Outlaw-fighters is what they are,

Doc. Been at it ever since the war ended, on the drift, forever ramblin', tanglin' with every kind of owlhoot trash you could name. I'm tellin' you them salty bucks have been just about everywhere and done just about everything."

"So this isn't their first saloon brawl," shrugged Beeby.

"Who could keep count?" Milt's grin was a fixture. "That's what I call *livin'*, Doc. Never a dull moment for Larry and Stretch."

"Count your blessings," growled Beeby. "You built J Bar from nothing. Now you're bossing one of the finest spreads in the territory, got a good loyal wife and three beautiful daughters, also a handsome bank account. So don't be regretting your lost youth, Milton Jacklin, and don't be envying a couple of tearaways like Valentine and Emerson."

"They do more livin' in a few months than most of us do in our whole lives," declared Milt.

Huddled under a table with his faro-dealer, the distraught Ritchie York wondered aloud,

"Why don't they come? What do we pay our law officers for?"

"It's Saturday night," the faro-dealer reminded him.

"You think I don't know that?" groaned York. "Of course it's Saturday — and payday! Why else would the town be crawling with high-spirited ranch-hands, all of 'em wrecking my place of business? Hell, if Hallam or his deputies don't soon put a stop to this, there'll be nothing left of the Queen of Diamonds!"

"This being Saturday night, the sheriff and the mayor'll be at Finley's pool hall," said the faro-dealer. "If Deputy Wright's on night patrol, he could be three blocks away. If Deputy Parry's playing poker in the back room at Mulligan's Bar, he won't hear anything — not even cannon-fire."

"How long does it take six booze-crazy cowhands to beat up just two strangers?" fumed York. "This fight shouldn't have lasted so long."

The faro-dealer warily edged his head out to check on the progress of the ruckus. Withdrawing it, he informed his boss,

"The strangers have taken a lot of punishment, but somehow they stay on their feet. You mightn't believe this, but Rube Madigan's hired hands are getting the worst of it."

"I don't care who wins or loses!" cried York. "I just want it over and done with — so we can start tallying the damage bill."

Nervously, he thrust his head out to scan the shambles that had once been a presentable barroom. The Texans were back to back now, fists flashing like pistons. He winced as Larry Valentine scored with an uppercut; the recipient demolished a table en route to the floor. Simultaneously, a man clobbered by the taller Texan was sent hurtling toward the batwings.

Deputy Chris Parry, not Deputy Billy

Wright, was patrolling the broad main street and drawing nearer the Queen of Diamonds when he became aware of a disturbance. What alerted the brawny Parry was the group cramming the sidewalk out front. The wild scatter of those onlookers was for the purpose of avoiding another human missile. Parry blinked incredulously as the Circle Nine man hit the outer edge of the sidewalk and bounced into the street.

"Stand aside!" he bellowed, brandishing his shotgun.

When he barged into the disheveled barroom, it was all over and the victors still upright, but panting heavily. He gawked at the tallest men ever seen in Kimber as they retrieved and donned their battered Stetsons. Larry Valentine of the heavy jaw and dark hair was brawnier than Parry and trimmer about the midriff, six feet three inches of husky Texan in travel-stained range rig, his ruggedly handsome visage showing a bruise or two, an abrasion or two. His partner, so aptly nicknamed, was taller again, topping him by three inches, a blond, shaggy-haired, homely beanpole who packed twice as much Colt as his sidekick.

Non-combatants were breaking cover and applauding, while the Circle Nine waddies lay where they had fallen. Milt Jacklin and Doc Beeby were emerging from behind the bar and York and his faro man rolling out from under a table. Lurching upright, the saloonkeeper raised his voice above the applause.

"Oh, hell, Parry! The damage — so much damage . . ."

Parry called for quiet and demanded to be told how the fight had started. Before Milt could speak up in defense of the Texans, the medico sourly complained,

"Some hotheads never know when to let up. My surmise is Madigan's men can't forget fathers and uncles who fought in the Union Army. A couple of southerners show up, and the damn fools start baiting them — just as though the war never ended."

"The war *hasn't* ended!" wailed York. "Damn it, Deputy, the Battle of Kimber City was fought in this saloon!"

"Circle Nine waddies started it, young Chris," grinned Milt. "These Texas boys didn't start swingin' till some jasper swung on them."

"Good enough for me," shrugged Parry, uncocking his shotgun. "I'm callin' for volunteers to help tote these losers to jail."

"To my surgery," corrected Beeby. "You blind, Chris? Look at 'em."

"Some helluva mess," nodded Parry.

"In an hour or so, you can lock 'em up," offered Beeby. "I think I can promise you they'll be in no condition to resist arrest."

"Haul 'em off to Doc's place," Parry ordered the volunteers.

"It'll take a week — maybe longer — to repair all this damage!" complained York.

"Keep your silk shirt on, Ritchie," soothed the deputy. "You know we got an ordinance covers this kind of situation. Rube Madigan's liable for damages. He'll pay the bills and take it out of the hired hands' pay."

"Madigan will also take care of *my* bill," Beeby said happily.

Milt now confronted the toilworn victors of that hectic set-to. He identified himself, offered a gnarled paw and declared it would be his pleasure, an honour in fact, to buy them a drink. In their present condition, they weren't about to reject such an invitation.

"But not here, Milt," insisted Larry.

"Hell, no, not here," Stretch said disdainfully. "We ain't drinkin' in a saloon so untidy."

"This place is a mess," complained Larry, while York gnashed his teeth.

"Disgustin', ain't it?" prodded Stretch.

"Disgustin'," agreed Larry. Then he vented his displeasure on the Circle Nine men, though they were befuddled and oblivious. "Damn dumbheads! Do we pick fights with northerners?"

"We don't pick fights with nobody,"

Stretch declared.

"So how come northerners want to beat our brains out — so long after the war?" scowled Larry.

"You boys could use a couple good stiff shots of bourbon," grinned Milt. "C'mon. I know a quieter place." A full five minutes after the J Bar boss quit the Queen of Diamonds with the tall strangers, the editor of the Kimber County 'Courier' arrived belatedly. Tubby Walt Kinstry was usually an active newsman quick to arrive on the scene of a commotion, but not tonight. A month ago he had taken a fall and broken a leg. Doc Beeby had expertly set and splinted the bone but, being no youngster, Kinstry couldn't expect to be rid of his crutch so soon after the accident.

"It must've been spectacular," he exclaimed, taken aback by the shambles of smashed furniture and broken glass. "And I had to miss it!"

"What've you got to whine about, Walt Kinstry?" York dolefully retorted.

"It wasn't your office got wrecked. That damn leg bone of yours'll heal and you'll be throwing that crutch away — by the time this place looks respectable again."

"The least somebody could've done was come fetch me," Kinstry chided the drinkers and staff. "Damn it, how long does it take to drive a buggy to my place, pick me up and fetch me back here?"

"Be thankful you weren't here, Walt," grinned a townman of his acquaintance. "The way your luck's running, you might've got hit by a chair."

The disgruntled newspaperman then demanded a blow by blow description of the affray from York and was invited to go break his other leg.

"No respect for the press," he complained, limping out again.

At a corner table of a small downtown bar, Milt Jacklin watched the living legends dab raw whiskey on facial gashes and skinned knuckles. They had taken a battering which, of course, could not be compared with the punishment inflicted on their attackers. They had emerged victorious; on the other hand they were in no mood to celebrate. They made it clear to their new friend that, given a choice, there would be no such muscle-wearying conflicts to disturb their peace.

"We talk of how peace-lovin' we are, and nobody believes it," grouched Stretch. "Hell, Milt, if you only knew."

"That's the truth?" Milt was intrigued. "You don't get no fun from fightin'?"

"If it was up to us, we'd never have to defend ourselves again," Larry sourly informed him. "How can it be fun? We've had our bellyful of it — for a long time."

"Way back when we quit Texas, we had our minds set on driftin' easy and havin' us a lazy life," muttered Stretch. "And the hell of it is . . ."

"It scarce ever happens," sighed Larry. "Either we keep runnin' into some kind of outlaw, or we just stop by a saloon for a quiet drink and a bunch of hotheads start crowdin' us. Why wouldn't we be weary of it, old timer? Wouldn't *you*?"

"I feel sorry for you boys," frowned Milt. "Don't seem fair. I mean, you've done so much for so many folks, risked your necks time and time again, fought and licked more outlaws than any lawman could handle, and what've you got to show for it?"

"Well, we don't need much," shrugged Larry. "Our horses and what we can tote is enough."

"Got no use for a fat bankroll," drawled Stretch. He drained his glass, nodded his thanks as Milt refilled it, then thought to enquire of his partner, "How much dinero we got anyway? I mean right now?"

"Better'n three hundred dollars," said Larry.

"For us, that's plenty," Stretch assured Milt.

"By damn." The veteran cattleman scratched his whiskers and surveyed them thoughtfully. "I've read a lot about you two, been admirin' you many a long year. Always knew, if I ever met up with you, it'd pleasure me to down a few shots of good whiskey with you. But now I'm thinkin' I could do better'n that. Damn right." He nodded emphatically. "Somethin' more important."

"You don't owe us no favors, Milt," said Larry.

"You'd be doin' *me* a favor," insisted Milt. "Top hands, ain't you? Born and raised in cattle country? Texas Panhandle, like it says in the papers." The drifters nodded, sipped whiskey and rolled cigarettes. "Well now, you could do somethin' for me *and* yourselves, and I'd pay regular ranch-hands' wage."

"Ain't lookin' for work right now," said Stretch.

"Lookin' for peace and quiet, right?" challenged Milt. "That's what I'm offerin', boys, all the peace and quiet you could hope for. You won't be around the spread and bunkin' and eatin' and workin' with my crew. You'll be by your own selves a long ways from my headquarters, way up in my north quarter, miles from anywhere."

Larry scratched a match on a thumbnail, touched flame to Stretch's cigarette, then his own, and eyed the old man longingly.

"Sounds too good to be true," he muttered.

"It's thisaway," Milt explained. "There's a piece of feed-range in my north quarter, sweetest graze you ever saw, and that's where I winter my best stock, hundred and fifty head, prime steers. Come round-up and after we make the drive to the railhead, it's them prime critters the cattle-buyers notice. J Bar herds never yet sold for less'n top dollar. So, you see, them critters're real special to me."

"Makes sense," nodded Larry.

"None of my hands mannin' the line shack up there right now," continued

Milt. "It's a four-bunk shack, but I had to empty it yesterday. These young cowpokes get bored, you know? Bein' stuck by Clear Creek through winter, they get to wranglin' and fightin' among 'emselves — damn fools that they are. I had to have Dan, my foreman, call 'em back in, else they'd have got to fightin' with knives or their six-shooters."

"Some fools can't appreciate solitude — peace and quiet," Stretch commented.

"You and Larry can," grinned Milt. "Exactly what you're cravin', huh?"

"It's startin' to sound good," mused Larry.

"It's better'n you'd guess," declared Milt. "You'd be there till spring, a cosy shack all to yourselves. Chores? Hell, scarce any chores. After sun-up, you check that little herd and any critters strayed to the brush east or the timber west, you just flush 'em out and run 'em back to the sweet graze where they belong. Outside of that, your time's your own. My regular hands gripe about it, claim it's too lonesome. *You* wouldn't. Right purty place, Clear Creek, this side of the Kimber Hills. Fishin's good. As for the shack, we keep improvin' on it. Roof don't leak and there ain't no cracks in them plank walls. Stove works fine, keeps the place warm and snug. Used to be just a corral for the horses. We built round it and roofed it too, so now it's a regular barn. By damn, there's a front porch even — with a couple rockin' chairs."

"And — uh — it's a long ways from any trail?" prodded Stretch.

"Better'n six miles from the stagecoach route," said Milt. "Nobody ever stops by the Clear Creek shack. That's why my fool hands get bored. They never see anybody but 'emselves."

"Runt," said Stretch. "I got a good feelin' about this."

"You and me both," Larry said fervently. "We'd be there two, maybe two and a half months . . ."

"Till spring," nodded Milt. "Gonna be an early spring this year, I reckon.

Creek's near thawed out, snow meltin' in the hills."

"Nothin' to do but nursemaid a little bitty herd, only a hundred and fifty of 'em," reflected Stretch. "Plenty time to flop and rest, runt. We live lazy till round-up time, don't see nobody 'cept just ourselves."

"Just one thing, Milt," said Larry. "We're new here, only rode in a few hours ago. You'd better tell us about Kimber County. Any ranchers feudin'? Any rustlin'?"

"We're all good buddies, me, Rube Madigan, Barney Garret, Quiddon, Sykes, Applegate, every ranchin' man in this territory," Milt assured him. "Hell, we can't remember how long ago we had rustler trouble. You can take it from me, Larry. You and Stretch hole up at Clear Creek, you'll have nothin' but peace the whole time you're there. And your horses'll be happy at J Bar. You can take 'em along if you want, but maybe you'd as soon they rest easy at the spread. We got a good string.

Take your pick, huh? Four good work critters, half-dozen if you'd rather."

"My horse earned himself a long spell, runt," said Stretch.

"Mine too," nodded Larry.

"I ain't stayin' in town tonight," said Milt. "Look, we could head on back to J Bar pretty soon, give you a chance to meet the wife and Dan and turn in early. Come mornin', the chuck-boss'll take you to Clear Creek. He'll load the wagon with enough grub to keep you eatin' steady and, by noon, you'll be there." He refilled their glasses and his own, eyeing them expectantly. "So what d'you say? We got a deal?"

"Easy livin'," grinned Stretch.

"Everything peaceful," Larry said wistfully.

"Just like we've been cravin'," Stretch reminded him.

"Cravin' — and never findin'," said Larry. "It's been a long time, amigo."

"Too long," declared Stretch. "How're we gonna say no to an offer so good?"

"We ain't sayin' no," grinned Larry.

"You got yourself a couple new hands, Milt. We'll tend the Clear Creek shack and your prime beeves and it'll be a pleasure."

"You won't regret this, boys," Milt promised.

After they quit that small bar, he retrieved his horse and accompanied them to the livery at which they had left their animals and gear. The stablehand was handsomely tipped, Larry's sorrel and Stretch's pinto saddled, packrolls slung and sheathed Winchesters secured, and then they were on their way to J Bar.

Upon their arrival at the Jacklin spread, the new hands were presented to Milt's amiable spouse and his taciturn but friendly enough foreman. Dan Corrie conducted them to a barn, watched them bed their animals down, then led them on to a bunkhouse. As he lit the lamp and indicated two empty bunks, he looked them over and tersely enquired,

"Anybody else know who Milt's just

hired? How about the local law?"

He was lean, leathery and shrewd-eyed, the kind of ramrod worthy of the respect of veteran trouble-shooters.

"We didn't tangle with the local law," Larry assured him.

"Just a half-dozen hotheads from a spread called Circle Nine," said Stretch.

"If you're as rough as I've heard," said Corrie, "Doc Beeby's still patchin' 'em."

"They'll be in the county calaboose by now," opined Larry. "They started it."

"Somebody else always starts it," said Stretch. "It's never us, Dan. We're plumb peaceable."

The ramrod grinned briefly.

"When the hands get back from their payday spree, they won't bother you none," he promised. "Sleep easy."

In the wee small hours, when the J Bar crew returned from the county seat, they were ordered to gather round the still-awake Dan Corrie. He ordered them to retire quietly, very quietly, especially the eight who slept in Number Two bunkhouse.

"No loud talk," he cautioned. "Tread soft and bunk down quiet. Couple new hands signed on last night. Sleepin' now. Mightn't take kindly to you waddies disturbin' 'em."

"Whatsamatter?" a bleary-eyed cowhand challenged. "Somethin' special about 'em?"

"Hear about the hullabaloo at York's place?" asked Corrie.

"Must've been some helluva hassle," mumbled another hand.

"The new men're the same two beat hell out of six Circle Nine rowdies," said Corrie.

Suitably impressed, also intimidated, the hands went to pains to retire quietly. With no disruptions, the battle-weary Texans slumbered on. And, while they slumbered, seven men of Northeast Nevada, some three hundred and fifty miles from Kimber County and the J Bar spread, held council on the project that had brought them together.

They were ruthless and devoid of conscience and united in a common commitment. That commitment was the murder of Larry Valentine and Stretch Emerson.

It was 3 a.m. Sunday morning when the three horsemen arrived at the small, rundown spread owned by one Jarvis Ames. The rancher and three of his cohorts were waiting in the house. Lamp-light glowed from the windows, a yellow, flickering welcome for the men dismounting beside the corrals. One of these, Lafe Hartigan, was the fifth man of this lonely cattle outfit. He was just returning from Twin Forks, the county seat, where his two companions had been identified and persuaded to accompany him.

Ames stood in the open doorway watching the three amble towards him. He was tall, lean and short-bearded, impassive most times. Some of his cronies had dubbed him Snake-Eyes; the cold grey eyes rarely blinked.

"Found 'em, Jarv," Hartigan called to him. "We've talked some, so they know Red Calnan was kin of mine." Reaching the porch, he indicated the two strangers. It was obvious they were brothers; the resemblance was striking. "Meet the Joad boys, Roy and Noah."

"Roy, Noah," Ames greeted the brothers quietly. "I understand you were pretty close to your cousin, Finn Garson?"

The Joads were some five years his junior, sharp-featured, wearing range clothes and packing Colts in tied-down holsters. Roy, the elder, gruffly assured him,

"We still mourn Cousin Finn."

"Come in," Ames invited. "Get comfortable."

The brothers followed Ames and Hartigan into a sizeable kitchen and claimed chairs. Hartigan lounged in the doorway. Squatting crosslegged on the floor, broad back resting against a plank wall, was the nondescript, denim-garbed Bob Furth, his face expressionless, a cigarette canting from the side of his mouth, a half-empty glass held in his left hand. Hartigan identified him for the newcomers, adding,

"Bob lost a brother."

"That's Clay Brandon," offered Ames, gesturing to the hulking, heavy-featured man slumped at the table.

Grim-eyed, Brandon told the Joads, "Your cousin died with my brothers."

"Ty Beavis lost a brother too," said Ames, indicated the slack-jawed character gnawing on a cold cigar. "Ty, our new friends look thirsty."

Beavis shoved a bottle at the Joads and said bitterly,

"Valentine busted Jed's head with a rifle butt."

"How about you?" Noah Joad challenged Ames.

"Kinsman of mine, Al Drood, will rot till he dies in the Kerrigan state pen," declared Ames, "thanks to Valentine and Emerson. I know you Joad boys have been hunting those heroes a long time. So has Lafe. So we all have the same cause, a score to settle with a couple of hot shot do-gooders who should've been eliminated years ago — fifteen years ago." He seated himself at the head of the table, lit a cigar and stared hard at the Joads. "I had Lafe find you because I've decided that we seven can succeed working together under my leadership. We'll succeed where so many others have failed — at the cost of their lives. We're gonna run the almighty Texas Trouble-Shooters to ground and, when we do, they'll never be heard of again, no more stories in the newspapers, no more glory for them. As well as finishing them, we'll bury them or leave their carcasses for the buzzards somewhere they'll never be found. That's the deal, boys."

"Count us in," Roy Joad said with relish.

"Seven — all with the same hunger." Hartigan chuckled elatedly. "Jarv, we're gonna do it!"

"Everbybody agreed?" demanded Ames. Six heads nodded. "So it begins here and now. First problem, how to find them."

"Here's where we trade what we know," Furth remarked to the brothers, "If we know anything."

Ames led off.

"They left Griddle Gulch after delivering some show people there, the Emma Cromwell troup. Can anybody add to that?"

"What we got to find out for starters," said Brandon, "is whichaway they traveled from Griddle Gulch."

"Go get it, Noah," urged the elder Joad. His brother downed another swig of rye, rose and moved out. Roy then announced, "We picked up a newspaper. It's two weeks old. The Hallsburg Herald."

"I've heard of Hallsburg," muttered Furth. "Northwest Utah I think."

"They were there, Valentine and Emerson?" frowned Ames.

"Just a while back," nodded Roy. "If we're lucky, they'll still be there."

"No chance," opined Hartigan. "They

never hang around that long."

The younger brother returned to offer the newspaper to Ames, who rifled through it and found the brief report of the famous outlaw-fighters' presence in the Utah township. Passages were read aloud for the benefit of Hartigan, Furth and Beavis.

"Currently resting in our fair city..." He grimaced contemptuously. "Messrs Valentine and Emerson, adventurers of great renown. Patronizing the games of chance at Morrison's North Star Saloon, enjoying the comforts of the Alcott Hotel."

"Paper's two weeks old," Roy said again.

"They'll be gone by the time we make Hallsburg," predicted Brandon.

"But we're bound to pick up a lead, so we can trail them from there," said Ames. "Lafe, come sun-up you'll deliver a message to Garth Baldwin." He was referring to a wealthy local rancher. "He wants this land, keeps making offers. Tell him I'll accept his last offer and am willing to clinch the deal before sundown. If he'll bring cash, I'll sign a receipt and a bill of sale, any necessary documents." He turned to the other men. "The cash from this sale, together with whatever cash the rest of you have, will take care of our traveling expenses."

"So we could be on our way . . . " began Furth.

"Headed for Utah inside forty-eight hours," nodded Ames.

"Has to be done," muttered Roy Joad. "They've been too long ridin' free and buildin' their big reputation."

"Everybody's heroes," sneered Brandon.

"That's what angers me," Ames said grimly. "Kin and friends of ours, good men beaten by those smart-aleck do-gooders, will be forgotten. Nobody cares about them, nobody but us. Valentine's forgotten them, I'm sure, Emerson too. It doesn't mean anything to them, just a few more of their victims gunned down or turned over to the law, a few more victories they'll be admired for."

"Really fazes you, huh?" Hartigan grinned and winked at Brandon. "But not just because your buddy Drood's stuck in a state pen, right? You got an older score to settle."

Ames turned beetroot-red. The unwinked eyes gleamed; a vein stood out on his temple. Huskily, he warned,

"Forget it, Lafe."

"Sure," shrugged Hartigan. "Whatever you say, friend."

"From now on, nothing is as important as our quest," Ames declared. "We'll not be intimidated by the lies and crazy exaggerations of newspapermen. Maybe it's true those heroes fight best when outnumbered, but they've never had to defend themselves against seven like us. I'll decide the time and place — and the way it's to be done."

"Then it'll be done," breathed Furth. "We'll do it right."

"Oh, sure." Brandon licked his lips. "Shot full of holes, bloody and dead, they won't look so unbeatable, the high and mighty Lone Star Hellions."

2

Winter Haven

AFTER breakfast Sunday morning, two J Bar rigs were readied. In front of the ranchhouse was the handsome surrey that would transport Milt Jacklin and his womenfolk to the Baptist chapel in Kimber County. Over by the cookshack and pointed northeast, its team in harness, was old Pike Gillerman's chuck-wagon into which Larry and Stretch were helping load the provisions for their late winter stint at Clear Creek.

Though still smarting from last night's hectic brawl and suffering some muscle-strain, the trouble-shooters worked cheerfully, insisted the frail and stooped chuckboss tote and load only the lightweight items. Their own horses were in for a well-earned spell at the ranch headquarters. They had chosen four sturdy animals from the J Bar string and saddled two; the other two would be led by tie-lines to their destination.

In his Sunday-best, Milt called to them from the ranch-house porch, repeating his assurance they would rest easy at 'the best damn line-shack in all of Kimber County.' They responded with genial nods and amiable grins. Old Milt was their kind of cattleman.

Off-duty hands had socialized with the tall men over breakfast, but warily, figuring any two sluggers who could beat the tar out of six of Circle Nine's toughest employees were not to be crossed by cowpokes valuing their dental equipment.

The Jacklin surrey departed for the county seat and, soon afterward, Pike Gillerman took his place on the seat of his wagon and the Texans swung astride. The journey north began, they riding level with the rig, leading the spare animals and admiring J Bar's lush green acres and the grazing herd.

"If you think them critters look prime, wait till you see the herd at the crick," drawled the chuckboss.

"Milt told us," nodded Larry. "Hundred and fifty of his best."

"Kinda lonesome up there," Pike warned.

"Milt told us that too," grinned Stretch. "Suits us fine, old timer. We wouldn't have it any other way."

"I mean plumb lonesome," stressed Pike. "You ain't gonna see nobody else but your own selves till Milt sends a passel of hands to fetch his prime beeves come round-up time. Gonna tell me you're all that partial to just your own company?"

"Stone cold truth," Stretch assured him. "All we need is us."

"We got used to each other," Larry told Pike. "And I mean a lot of years back."

"Well now, one thing's for sure," offered Pike. "You'll be cosy enough, by golly. Plenty firewood in the shack and plenty more in the timber west. Stove's near brand-new, works just fine. You got all the comforts of home, boys. Milt tell you there's a front porch?" They nodded. "Three-hole privy out back too. Why, there's even a root cellar."

"A root cellar," enthused Stretch. "Think of that."

"We sunk her way back when the shack was first built," recalled Pike. "Trapdoor's a few feet from the stove. That old root cellar, well, I'm tellin' you everything stays cool down there. Ain't good for just storin' vegetables and meat. Right handy place for liquor. You'll find a keg of rum, best thing for warmin' your innards on a cold night. Couple of kegs of good whiskey too." He shook his head irritably. "Danged if I can savvy why so many of our hands get to wranglin' with one another in such a peaceful place, but it always happens. Dan Corrie figures it's the monotony. Milt say it's on accounta they ain't got no imagination, dunno how to keep their brains workin' — what brains they got."

"They could both be right," suggested Larry.

"Guess so," shrugged Pike. "Tell me a thing. You boys any good with them Winchesters?"

"Passable," Larry said modestly.

"Seein' as how spring's comin' early, you might get in some huntin'," said Pike. "Never know your luck. Deer maybe. I've seen quail in them hills too. You got fish lines?"

"We got fish lines," said Stretch, grinning in anticipation.

"Time'll pass too fast for us, Pike," declared Larry. "Plain truth is we *need* a place like Clear Creek. We've been too blame busy for too damn long."

"Ain't that the truth," Stretch agreed.

"Heard about the fight," said Pike. "Them Circle Nine waddies give you a bad time?"

"We're still hurtin'," confided Larry.

"Uh huh," grunted Pike. "Well, if it's true what Milt told me — and he don't lie — you didn't get the worst of it."

"We just do the best we know how," shrugged Stretch.

He traded grins with his partner. They liked everything they saw in this verdant terrain, the vast J Bar herd, the green flats almost devoid of snow and ice, the lingering chill of winter more invigorating than discomforting. This was the life for them — when they could find it. And it had been a long time coming.

So extensive was the land owned by Milt Jacklin, it was almost noon before they sighted the shack and its surrounds, the majestic stand of timber to the west, the good graze to the east with, further east, a line of brush and, between the shack and the brush, 150 head, Milt's best stock, the rippling creek only a short distance north with, beyond, the draws and rises of the Kimber Hills. Paradise, they reflected. Solitude aplenty. Here, their peace would be undisturbed. Here, they would relax, the old tensions easing, the nerve-wracking battles with a hundred and one homicidal outlaws forgotten.

They grinned eagerly at the rockers on the porch while toting supplies into the shack. The interior was as Milt had described it, proof against the elements, the stove in good order, the table and chairs sturdy, the bunks comfortable-looking. Stretch raised the cellar trapdoor and elected to stow the perishables down there. The ladder, he found, didn't groan under his weight; it was as sturdy as the plank floor and the shingled roof.

"We got no fixin' to do here," he remarked to Larry. "Everything works fine."

"Might's well eat 'fore I head back," Pike decided. "I'll rustle up lunch, show you boys how the stove works, after you bed them saddle-animals."

The horses were bedded in the barn, the well and privy tested and the last box of provisions unloaded, after which Pike cooked and dished up a mouth-watering meal, Stretch following his practiced movements, Larry lounging in the doorway and surveying the area east and south. In his swing toward the shack, Pike had driven clear of a rampart of tall boulders some forty yards away. The only other rocks visible were away east just this side of the brush, and north at the base of the hills beyond the creek. The graze accommodating the prime steers was a carpet of green perfect for the fattening of top grade stock. But, cattle being what they were, they would stray.

"Let 'em stray," he mused aloud. "Flushin' 'em out of the brush or the trees is gonna be dead easy."

"Sure," nodded Pike. "Easy chore for any jasper savvies cattle. Come eat, son."

After that fine lunch, the aged chuckboss returned to his rig and, trading farewells with the new hands, kicked off the brake and wheeled his team southward. The Texans watched till the vehicle was lost from view, then sighed contentedly, flopped into the porch chairs and fished out their makings. They grinned at each other.

"How about this, huh?" drawled Larry.

"We finally made it, runt," declared Stretch.

"Peace and quiet," muttered Larry. "You hear any guns, any booze-brave hotheads cussin' us, any poor sonofagun yellin' for our help?"

"I don't hear nothin' but the birds a 'twitterin' and the creek a'flowin'," Stretch said wistfully.

"That's what peace sounds like," said Larry. "Now you know."

"We deserve this," asserted Stretch.

"I can't think of any two hombres deserve it more," said Larry. They lit their after-lunch smokes. He raised his boots to the porch-rail, slumped lower and decided, "After a while, when I get to feelin' the urge, I'll take my time saddlin' a critter and go tally the herd."

"Takin' your time." Stretch nodded approvingly.

"Well, sure," nodded Larry. "No rush. And any that's strayed, I'll go find 'em and run 'em back to graze. Take my time about that too."

"This is the life for us," said Stretch. "Worth waitin' for, huh?"

"Worth waitin' for," Larry fervently agreed.

While the Texans were relaxing at J Bar's north line shack, the wife and brother of the founder-editor of the Kimber County 'Courier' were sipping coffee and doggedly doing likewise. They had learned to relax, Clara Kinstry and her brother-in-law Eric, through Walt Kinstry's difficult period of disability. Placid Clara had decided her husband had nobody but himself to blame. No patience, no gratitude for small mercies. Well, he might have broken both legs, an arm also, so why did he have to be so irascible?

It had been another excellent lunch, typical of the fare prepared and served by Clara with the help of her niece.

Now they lingered over their coffee, her husband grouching, her niece eyeing him reproachfully. A nice young lady, Inez Durley, orphaned daughter of Clara's sister and her husband, no outstanding beauty by any means, but of pleasing countenance and neat of figure, a pleasant person, but often awkward and not just physically; she too often lacked tact when dealing with her Uncle Walt's irritable disposition.

"York's place practically wrecked, a brawl of great vigor and violence," he grouched. "And me not there to see it, unable now to write a first-hand account of it. And why? Because I'm slowed down by this leg!"

His brother spoke up, but mildly. Eric Kinstry was indispensable around the Courier office, Walt's righthand man and, in his own unobtrusive way, extremely versatile. He could write copy, compose classified ads, set type, work the press and keep it operational.

"If I'd heard of it, Walt, I'd have hustled along to the Queen of Diamonds.

But, as you know, the press had broken down and ... "

"Yeah, you had chores," nodded Kinstry. "Everything fixed now?"

"Working well," said Eric.

"I have no sympathy with you, Uncle Walter," Inez said aloofly, while her aunt wished she hadn't. "You could have sent me and, had you done so, you would now have a complete report of the incident."

"Send you to a saloon?" scowled Kinstry.

"From the entrance I'd have been able to observe, or from a window," she declared. "No need for me to enter the barroom."

"Peeking through a window you could've become *another* casualty," he retorted.

"Somebody told me a Circle Nine rowdy crashed through a window into the side alley," offered Eric. "Till after midnight, Doc Beeby was removing slivers of glass from his — well, I won't say which part of him. Ladies present."

"See what I mean?" Kinstry growled at his niece. "It was no place for you, young woman. As for any report you'd have written, the Courier couldn't use it. You've no more talent for journalism than for fiction — you with your pie in the sky notions of becoming a novelist."

"You are jealous of my abilities," she accused.

"*What* abilities?" he sneered.

"Now, Walt, give the child her due," smiled Clara. "She does beautiful needlework at Mrs McEvoy's store and helps me with the cooking and housework."

"She's a part-time seamstress for Sophie McEvoy," growled Kinstry. "She is also a calamity in skirts and full of foolish aspirations." He shook a finger at his niece. "Leave the writing of novels to Jane Austen and the Bronte sisters. You pestered me to read your manuscripts and read 'em I did and, if you know what's good for you, you'll heed my advice. A writer you'll never be. Your mind and your pen run away with you. Imagination is essential, sure. But too much imagination is an irritation to readers, almost as irritating as your over-use of adjectives and your long-winded descriptive passages, not to mention the boring dialogue."

"My literary style is developing," Inez serenely assured him. "Say what you will, Uncle Walter, I cannot be discouraged by your caustic criticism."

"Wasn't the rejection of two manuscripts — from publishers all over the country — proof enough for you?" he challenged. "Inez Marigold Durley, you'd better believe it's a wise amateur knows when to quit. What you write is romantic, fanciful, unconvincing hogwash."

"Stick and stones," cooed Inez.

"Don't lose your temper, Walt dear," begged Clara. "Remember you're not a well man."

"What in thunderation are you talking about?" he demanded. "I didn't suffer a heart seizure. I broke a leg."

"I just thought — I ought to say something," she said lamely.

"If you had any sense," Kinstry chided his niece, "you'd give up on your crazy ideas of writing a best selling novel and show Damien Blackwood some encouragement. You're being courted by a mighty eligible bachelor, the best prospect in Kimber City, and he deserves some appreciation, doesn't he?"

"Chief cashier at the Merchants and Settlers Bank, Inez dear," smiled Clara. "When Mister Howell retires, Damien's bound to replace him as manager."

"My career comes first," said Inez. "I admire Damien of course but, if he really loves me, he'll be patient and wait. After I become an established writer, I'll reconsider his proposal."

"Doesn't it bother you that you're near twenty-two and still a spinster?" jibed Kinstry. "Your aunt was seventeen and I wasn't yet of age when we married. See how happy *she* is — married to a decent, sweet-natured, patient man like me?"

"My career comes first," repeated Inez.

"Bunkum!" jeered Kinstry.

The remainder of that Sunday was restful for the new occupants of the line shack at Clear Creek. Larry's unhurried tally proved every animal of Milt Jacklin's prime stock was right where it was supposed to be. He and Stretch collaborated at cooking a handsome, supper, downed every mouthful, tidied up, spent a half-hour lazing on the porch and, when the temperature dropped, retreated into the shack, stoked up the fire, chose bunks and called it a day.

Monday morning around 11 o'clock the tranquility was prevailing. Five head had strayed to the brush in the early morning; it took Stretch less than a quarter-hour to flush them back to the main bunch. They were again relaxing on the porch, enjoying a companionable silence, when Larry grimaced and cocked an ear.

"Nothin'," Stretch said uneasily. "Just a rider."

"Milt and Dan said it and so did old Pike," scowled Larry. "Nobody else ever comes here. We'd have the place to ourselves."

"Sounds like just one rider," shrugged Stretch.

"We only got here noon yesterday," grouched Larry. "It's supposed to be peaceful for us — nobody comin' by till near round-up time."

"Just one rider," Stretch repeated, wincing.

"Comin' on fast and headed our way," complained Larry, glancing northward.

"Mightn't know we're here," offered Stretch.

"He knows somebody's here," retorted Larry. "Smoke from our chimney's guidin' him to us."

"Hey." Stretch rose hastily. "It ain't a him."

The rider was female and beautiful, a blonde woman emerging from the hills at full gallop, not slowing the pace when she put her calico gelding to the creek. She was hatless, Larry noted, blonde hair streaming.

"Rides sidesaddle and rides good," he observed.

"Nice duds she's wearin'," said Stretch, squinting.

She was fording fast, the calico raising spray. Larry saw her look back over her shoulder as he informed his partner.

"It's called a ridin' habit."

"Why do they call it that?" demanded a puzzled Stretch. "Hell, I've had the ridin' habit since I was knee-high."

"Your guess is as good as mine," shrugged Larry.

From the south bank, the woman rode fast to the shack to bring her mount to a panting halt. The beautiful face was flushed, the blue eyes wide with fear. She dismounted quickly and appealed to them.

"Please — you have to help me — to protect me! They're chasing me . . . !"

"How many of 'em?" frowned Larry.

"Three," she told him. "I'm terrified!

They — they're *fiends*!"

"I'll put the horse in the barn, runt," muttered Stretch, after a wary glance toward the creek. "The lady'd better . . . "

"Yeah." Larry jerked a thumb as Stretch descended to take the calico's rein. "Inside, lady."

"They're *fiends*!" she cried again, dashing into the shack. He reached in to pull the door shut and, when Stretch rejoined him, was propping a shoulder against a porch post and watching the area beyond the creek. He was disgruntled, but no more so than his partner, who remarked in disgust,

"Real peaceable territory. Decent female can't go a' ridin' without runnin' into skirt-chasers."

"Three of 'em, she says," growled Larry.

"We can handle 'em," shrugged Stretch.

"We can handle 'em, sure," nodded Larry. "But that ain't what we're here for."

"Don't seem fair," complained Stretch, cocking an ear to the urgent drumming of hooves.

A few moments later and the three horsemen were out of the hills and in clear sight of the Texans, charging their mounts across the creek. Stretch observed they were mean hombres and won no argument from Larry. Three hefty, roughly-garbed men, bearded, beligerent.

Reining up after tracking the calico to the shack, the eldest of the three swung down and glowered at the Texans. There was grey in his beard and at his temples, but Larry saw him as a force to be reckoned with; he was broad-shouldered and muscular.

"If you waddies know what's good for you, don't get in our way," was his opening gambit. His eyes, red-rimmed with fury, switched to the closed door. At the top of his voice, he called his demand. "Come on outa there, consarn you!"

"Forget it," said Larry.

"Don't tell me forget it!" the big man snarled, moving forward.

Up the three steps he barged, his thick arms out-thrown in what proved to be a futile attempt to shove the tall men aside. One-handed, Larry grasped him by a shoulder, turned him and shoved. A bull-like roar of rage rose on the late morning air as he pitched to the dust, sprawling on face and hands. The other two promptly loosed threatening growls, dismounted and charged the porch and, by then, the Texans were descending, ready and willing to defend themselves. Larry ducked a clumsy swing, drove left fist into a belly and right fist at a bewhiskererd jaw, while Stretch blocked a roundhouse right and retaliated with a nose-bloodying jab that sent his would-be assailant reeling back to the first man, who had begun picking himself up. The collision triggered howls of fury; the eldest of the invaders was down again, pinned by Bloody-Nose. The other man tried Larry again and paid for it. This time, Larry's left bounced off the side of his head and spun him to the hard ground.

"By all the saints ... " gasped the older man, "this'll mean war 'tween me and Milt Jacklin! Any neighbor that'd meddle in Quiddon family business ain't no friend of mine any more!"

"What the hell're you talkin' about?" challenged Larry.

"You're helpin' her!" The big man finally made it to his feet and pointed accusingly. "She's tryin' to run away from her family — my own daughter — to take up with a lowdown card-sharpin' tinhorn!"

Stretch's jaw sagged. Larry now thought to study the brands of the three horses, a Q in a box.

"Lady on the calico's your daughter?" he frowned. "We didn't know that. Damn and blast, we're new in this territory."

"I'm Enoch Quiddon. These're my boys, Newt and Luther — and I sired her too, that sassy brat!" Quiddon was seething. He raised his voice again.

"Marcie, come on outa there!"

Son Luther of the bloody and fast-swelling nose, lurched upright panting.

"Soon as I — catch my wind..." he warned the taller Texan, "I'm gonna bust your snoot worse'n you busted mine."

"Hold on now, gents," pleaded Stretch. "Little misunderstandin' here. It's all a mistake."

"Biggest mistake *I* ever made by payin' good money to buy that fool girl-child a high-falutin' education!" complained Quiddon. "Now she's fulla big ideas, thinks we ain't good enough for her! Well, damn her sass, no Fancy Dan sharper's good enough for *her*!"

"She just rode in scared and claimed three bad hombres were chasin' her," Larry said apologetically. "Look, if we'd known..."

He clenched his teeth, his ire aroused by the screamed protest from inside the shack; Marcie Quiddon indignantly asserted,

"I've never seen those men before in my life!"

"Shuddup and get out here!" roared Quiddon.

"You're welcome to her, friend," muttered Larry. "But you don't have to bust in. I'll fetch her out — when I'm through with her."

"When you're — what?" Son Newt asked suspiciously. "What's he mean, Pa?"

"This won't take but a minute," promised Larry.

With that, he climbed the steps, crossed the porch, opened the door and disappeared inside. The door was swung shut after which the brothers stared aghast at their sire and an uncomfortable Stretch made placating gestures. Marcie Quiddon's screams reached the red ears of her father and brothers with harrowing clarity. The screams became yelps, the yelps keeping time with a steady pounding sound all too familiar to Stretch. Oh, hell. Larry was doing it again.

"What's he *doin'* to her?" demanded Newt.

"Nothin' real bad," Stretch earnestly assured him. "She won't die of it."

Quiddon's eyes narrowed.

"Stand clear of that door," he ordered, starting for the steps again. "She's my daughter. I got a right to see what's happenin'."

"No need to bust the door, Mister Quiddon suh," mumbled Stretch, reaching to the knob. "Be glad to open up for you. And there ain't nothin' happenin' to the lady that oughtn't have happened before — often."

He opened the door and entered. Quiddon and his sons progressed only as far as the threshold. From there, they gawked at the seated Larry and the loudly protesting woman thrown across his lap and his right hand rising and falling, the flat of it never missing its shapely target.

"Pa, he's molestin' her!" gasped Luther. "He's paddlin' her butt!"

"And she's got it comin'," growled

the master of Box Q.

Abruptly, Larry rose and deposited the crimson-cheeked Marcie to her feet. He then cut short her tirade by sternly warning her,

"Don't never lie to me or my partner again, hear?"

"You — despicable roughneck!" she gasped.

"Somethin' you better know about us," declared Larry. "We never yet failed a woman needin' help. If you came by to water your horse we'd treat you hospitable and, if your horse was lame with a rock stuck in his hoof, we'd dig it out."

"Fix coffee for you, anything at all," offered Stretch.

"We'll be mighty polite and help any way we can," Larry assured her. "But don't never lie to us!"

"Aren't you going to punish him?" she challenged her father. "You saw what he did to me!"

"I saw — and it looked good to me," scowled Quiddon. "And now I'm tellin' you for the last time, you pesky wildcat. Stay far clear of Ace Healey. Save yourself for a real man, not a dud cardsharp."

"That dude won't be around Kimber much longer anyway," opined Newt. "He'll get himself run outa town, nothin' surer."

"Where's her horse, the calico?" demanded Quiddon.

"In the leant-to, Mister Quiddon suh, and I'll be glad to fetch it," said Stretch. He nodded affably to the brothers. "'Scuse me."

They stood aside. He moved out and, a few moments later, the calico was rump to rump with the other Box Q animals and the rancher hustling his daughter out of the shack. Gingerly, all the time glaring at Larry, she remounted. Her father and sons climbed astride. And then, just before heading for the creek with his children, Quiddon challenged the tall men. Were they new J Bar hands or just drifters making use of the line shack?

"He's Woodville, I'm Lawrence," offered Larry. "Milt signed us on to tend his prime steers till round-up time." He added respectfully, "We're sorry about this. But, like I said, we just didn't know."

"And we're real sorry we had to hurt you gents," Stretch said contritely.

"It ain't fair, Pa," mumbled Luther. "We're hurtin' all over — but they ain't hurt at all."

"Well ... " Larry eyed the beautiful blonde coldly. "My right hand smarts some."

"We'll be headin' home now," frowned Quiddon. "Uh — I got just one last question. You the same two sluggers beat hell outa a half-dozen of Rube Madigan's bunch at the Queen of Diamonds?"

"They didn't give us any choice," shrugged Larry.

"We're sorry about that too," said Stretch.

The rancher almost grinned as he muttered a retort.

"Not as sorry as Madigan's boys, I'll bet."

Beginning their journey back to Box Q, the four riders forded Clear Creek unhurriedly. The Texans stared after them, Larry blowing on his tingling right palm, Stretch waxing optimistic.

"This was just somethin' never happened before, runt. We oughtn't fret about it. I mean, you just *know* it couldn't happen again."

"I wish I could count on it," said Larry. He grimaced resentfully. "That high-falutin' female. If she's hexed us, it'll cost her. I might just paddle her ass again."

Late afternoon of the following day, a deputy sheriff of Twin Forks, Nevada, sought his boss and found him filling his favorite window chair at his favorite saloon. There were only a few years between Art Scott and Sheriff Joshua Leyland; both were veteran law officers.

"You're gonna be interested," Scott predicted, seating himself. "Something

I just found out, Josh. Knew you'd want to know. It's about that hard case bunch you're leery of — Ames and his buddies?"

Leyland stroked his baggy jowls and shifted his gaze from Main Street, Twin Forks, to his deputy's face.

"Damn right I'm interested," he muttered. "Let's hear it."

3

Memories of Jake Tyne

THE deputy dealt it out tersely. "Ames isn't ranching that piece of county any more. He's sold out to Garth Baldwin and quit, and he didn't ride out alone."

"Took his four sidekicks along?" frowned Leyland. Scott nodded. "Good riddance. Don't know about the others, but Clay Brandon did a hitch in the San Remo pen, we know that for a fact. As for Ames, I never trusted him anyway."

"A few nights back, the Joad brothers were in Twin Forks," said Scott. "I saw Lafe Hartigan parleying with 'em."

"Hartigan," grimaced Leyland. "Another of Ames's pals."

"They rode out together," said Scott. "We got a file on the Joad boys, but nothing we could hold 'em on. Two arrests far west of here, no convictions. They had to be turned loose, Josh."

"Lack of evidence," nodded Leyland.

"Couple of real mean ones, those Joads," muttered Scott. "And now I'm pretty sure they're headed someplace with the Ames bunch. Carey, Baldwin's foreman, saw 'em headed east out of the county. Not five of 'em. Seven."

"So they're long gone from my bailiwick," mused Leyland. "We can forget 'em, Art, but now I'm thinking of one man who'll never forget Jarvis Ames."

"I know who you mean," said Scott. "Brad Tyne."

"Doesn't carry a badge nowadays, last I heard," said Leyland. "Got to be too mean a lawman after his old man was gunned down by bank-robbers in Beauvais, Utah. Jake was town marshal there, young Brad was his deputy. The boss-thief was masked — it was him shot Jake — but Brad still suspects Ames was the killer, claimed the man moved like Ames and used the kind of handgun Ames favors, a Smith & Wesson forty-four."

"Many a man owns one," Scott said dubiously. "Might be young Brad just *wanted* to believe it."

"And it might be he's right," Leyland retorted. "Ames had money when he came here. No fortune, but enough to start his own spread."

"As well as turning mean, didn't Brad hit the bottle kind of?" asked Scott.

"His mother died a couple months after Jake's funeral," said Leyland. "I guess losing Jake just broke her heart. There weren't any other's born of that marriage. The boy was close to his folks, so maybe he fell apart. But I don't think the booze licked him, Art. No saloonkeeper would hire a tableman who couldn't hold his liquor."

"How'd you find out about that?" demanded Scott.

"Whiskey drummer of my acquaintance came through here last week," said Leyland. "Picked up a few orders in

Beauvais and that's where he saw Brad Tyne, cold sober and running the faro games in the biggest saloon in town, the Chestnut. No drunk can deal a game of chance, especially faro."

"You got something on your mind," opined Scott, eyeing him intently.

"Maybe I'd be doing him no favor," mused Leyland. "I just have this feeling somebody ought to tip him off, let him know Ames is on the move again — and with the Joad boys siding him. Ever heard it said, Art? Once a lawman, always a lawman."

"Your decision," shrugged Scott. "Come to think of it, there'll be an eastbound stage picking up mail here tomorrow. Beauvais is on the Collins Line's route. So, if you're thinking of writing Tyne ... "

"Plenty time," remarked Leyland. "I'll write the letter tonight." He grinned reminiscently. "Can't recall if I ever mentioned."

"What?" asked Scott.

"I knew Jake Tyne well," said

Leyland. "He was a friend, Art, I mean a real friend. We were deputies together, backed up Dakota Dave Mulligan in the old days. Oh, yes. We go back, Jake and me."

"You said maybe it'll be no favor to Jake's boy," said Scott.

"Jake claimed Brad was a good and steady deputy," muttered Leyland. "I don't reckon he'll do anything rash. At least I hope he won't. But he has a right to know. So, yes, I'll write him tonight."

When Marcie Quiddon next visited the county seat, she wasn't allowed the opportunity to seek out the handsome gambler with whom she was infatuated. She traveled in with her mother in the family surrey driven by Andy Starrett, the Box Q foreman. An alert-eyed veteran, Andy Starrett; he didn't miss much.

Chloe Quiddon and her daughter, in town for some marketing, were in Pringle's general emporium when

Inez Durley entered. It happened that Inez and Marcie were close friends, so the inevitable excited greetings were exchanged, while Andy Starrett loitered by the cracker barrel and Chloe chose cloth and thread.

"So much to tell you," gushed Marcie. "I've had the most terrible, the most humiliating experience."

"Poor Marcie, you must be so upset about that gambler you were getting to know," Inez sympathized.

"Ace?" frowned Marcie. "What about him?"

"I'm sorry, apparently you've not heard," said Inez. "Just yesterday afternoon, he was ordered to leave town. It seems he was not exactly an honest gambler, Marcie. He was caught cheating and Sheriff Hallam was advised — and now he's gone."

"Another broken romance!" Marcie Quiddon had a fondness for the melodramatic. To Starrett's amusement, she raised back of hand to brow and sighed heavily. "I'm virtually a prisoner,

Inez, under constant surveillance of my father and brothers."

"I can do so little to comfort you, poor Marcie, except visit you now and then," said Inez.

"Don't come now and then," begged Marcie. "Come often — please? I declare I'm starved for stimulating conversation. You're my only contact with civilization, Inez dear. And, fortunately, Mother and even my surly father approve of you."

"I'll be out to Box Q as soon as I can make time," promised Inez.

"It was just ghastly, the morning of my escape — my so brief escape," complained Marcie. "I wanted so much to see Ace again and, no sooner had I ridden off Box Q range than Father and both my brothers were in hot pursuit. I tried to elude them by detouring through the hills, but didn't." She went on to recount the incident at the line shack, the indignity she had suffered at the hands of a ruffianly stranger — especially his right hand. The brawl was described in graphic detail, as were the new men guarding Jacklin's Clear Creek range. And, to round off the account, she expressed her disgust that her father seemed almost to admire them, despite the rough treatment he had suffered. "Uncouth roughnecks, Inez. He's no gentleman, the one called Lawrence. And the other, Woodville, is a gangling clumsy oaf."

Inez managed to control her mounting excitement.

"You say they were quite tall?" she frowned.

"Ridiculously tall, the tallest I've ever seen," Marcie said disdainfully. Then she hugged her friend and repeated her pleas. "You will come visit me — soon?"

"Very soon," nodded Inez.

After finishing her chores at Sophie McEvoy's ladies store that morning, she walked the three blocks to the newspaper office in a mood of eager anticipation. Suddenly her hometown with its busy business sector and the residential streets angling off the main thoroughfare seemed a brighter, more exciting place. A golden opportunity had been presented to her, unless she were mistaken. 'But it couldn't be a mistake,' she reflected. 'Marcie was so sure of the names they gave to her father, Lawrence and Woodville. I'm sure those names are important, but can't remember why. No matter. I have only to check Uncle Walter's back issues and jog my memory.'

Before lunch, while her elder uncle was out of the office and her younger uncle setting type and paying no attention to her, she rummaged through stacks of old editions and found the Courier's front page story of the assassination attempt on Vice President Jordan Barclay foiled by those famous Texas drifters, Lawrence Valentine and Woodville 'Stretch' Emerson. She resisted the impulse to loose a squeal of triumph. Oh, this was an opportunity and no mistake. And nobody else, including her news-conscious uncle and Sheriff Hallam himself, suspected the identity of the men hired to man the Clear Creek line shack.

The plan formed in her mind while she helped her aunt prepare lunch. At the first opportunity, she would visit her dear friend Marcie at the Box Q ranch. It would be a short visit, after which she would make her way to the shack by way of the Kimber Hills. The notorious trouble-shooters, known to be suspicious of the fourth estate, would be kept in ignorance of her relationship to the editor of the county paper. She would ingratiate herself, get to know them and observe them, but would be careful to take no notes in their presence.

'Store it all in my mind, the retentive mind of a brilliant writer,' she decided. 'Then write a profile of the West's most famous adventurers, yes, a searching analysis, the definitive work on Larry and Stretch, the living legends. What kind of persons are they really? Are they as uncouth as Marcie claims or have they a gentler side? Are they proud of their achievements, the hundreds of law-breakers they've brought to justice, or will I find them to be modest, self-effacing? I must work in secret of course, not a word to Uncle Walter till I'm ready to mail the manuscript. I may then permit him to read it and, *this* time, he'll be *forced* to acknowledge my talent!'

Some days later, Jarvis Ames and his cohorts reached Hallsburg, in the Utah Territory, purchased supplies, asked questions and, having learned the date of the trouble-shooters' departure from that town and the direction they had traveled, resumed their hunt. Bradford Tyne of the Chestnut Saloon at Beauvais had received Sheriff Josh Leyland's letter and was, at this time, reading it for the fifth time. It was early afternoon, a few drinkers at the bar, but none showing interest in the games of chance. Tyne was, in his twenty-sixth year, an unsmiling man some might call handsome, his neat mustache matching a well-barbered mane of light brown hair, his compact five feet eleven inches garbed in the well-tailored rig of the typical faro dealer.

To Hildy Fitzgerald's way of thinking, he was attractive and more, she was in love with him and he knew it. He also knew her to be patient, discreet and of above average intelligence. The sister of his boss was no decorative hanger-on. She helped run the place, could keep the accounts, entertain customers singing to her own accompaniment and fill in at dealing poker or supervising the roulette layout.

He was still reading when she brought two cups of coffee to his table. She moved with grace, a fine-figured woman whose clinging green gown emphasized her fair complexion and auburn hair. He grunted his thanks, pocketed the letter and rose to help her be seated.

"It's fresh, I just made it." Hildegarde Margaret Fitzgerald made herself comfortable and surveyed him steadily. "You have that look in your eye again, that far-away look. Still remembering, are you?"

"Hildy," he said. "It's not all that long since it happened. Some Beauvais know-it-alls claim the two deaths left me a little crazy, but I think you and Pete know better."

"It's not madness, just grief and resentment," she opined. "I can understand it, though it was different for Pete and me. We were very young when our parents died. You lost your father — then your mother — in such a tragic way." She sipped coffee and murmured apologetically, "Sorry. I'm opening old wounds."

"No," he said. "You're the only one I can talk to."

"You know how I feel about you," she said. "Just don't let it bother you, all right? I'm not pushing it, Brad. I'd rather wait till you can smile again and you can't do that while your memories are so clear — and so bitter."

"In the heart or the head would have been more merciful," Tyne said grimly. "Two belly-wounds, Hildy. It was a slow and painful way for him to go, and the man who shot him *knew* that."

"You were never able to prove the killer's identity," she said. "All you have is suspicion."

"It was Ames's style," he declared. "Somebody talked about him, Hildy, a gunslinger I nailed a year and a half ago."

"Steve Butler," she nodded. "I remember."

"Butler and Ames were in cahoots at one time," he said. "So Butler really knew him. I can quote his very words. 'A streak of evil. I've ridden with some heartless jaspers and I'm telling you Ames is the worst.' There'll never be any doubt in my mind, Hildy. It was Ames shot my father. And watching him die was more than my mother could bear."

"You'll keep right on torturing yourself," she sighed.

He downed a mouthful of coffee and

shook his head irritably.

"This isn't fair to you. I oughtn't burden you with it."

"What're friends for?" She smiled wryly. "Go ahead. Burden me."

"Let me ask you something," he said. "Do you suppose Pete would keep my job open if I had to leave town a while?"

"How long a while?" she asked.

"Weeks, maybe months," he shrugged.

Her face clouded over.

"It's something to do with that letter," she frowned. "I don't pry, but I couldn't help noticing — you seem to be always reading it."

"This you can believe," he assured her. "I'm not about to play lone avenger. Somebody has given me a lead. I want to follow up on it, but I still think as a lawman. Wherever this lead takes me, I'll be going by the book, checking with the chief law officers of every town I visit."

"No use my asking questions," she said sadly. "You won't appreciate questions, so I'll just beg."

"You don't have to ... " he began.

"I'm begging anyway," she said. "Whatever you intend doing, control your emotions, please? No unnecessary risks. Take care of yourself. For your own sake, Brad, if not for mine."

"You have my word," he muttered. "Now how about Pete?"

"Only one way to find out," she said. "He's in his office right now. Go ask."

He drained his cup, got to his feet and, for a brief moment, let his hand rest on her shoulder. Then he hurried to the stairs and, left alone, the sensitive-featured redhead brooded on the never-to-be-forgotten bank robbery of recent times. It was all clear in her mind, she having witnessed some of the action. From the saloon entrance, frozen with shock, she had watched four masked men emerge from the bank to dash to the horses held by a fifth man. Marshal Jake Tyne had then appeared, advancing from the east along the main street while his deputy son approached from the west. Brad was a full block and a half away when he saw his father gunned down by the boss-bandit. Then the robbers were mounted and in flight, townfolk frantically scattering for cover and Brad yelling in grief and fury, dashing to a hitch-rail to whisk a rifle from the scabbard off a horse tethered there, triggering a burst after the fleeing bandits, missing the leader but scoring on the tag-rider. The man fell with a bullet in his head, died instantly and was never identified. While kneeling by his pain-wracked father, waiting for the local doctor to answer his summons, Brad had questioned a cashier as to the way the boss-bandit moved, the make of handgun he used, the manner in which the holster was slung.

Brad would have inherited his dead father's badge, had grief and frustration not driven him to drink. For a short time, a pitifully short time, he stayed on the job as the new marshal's deputy, a drinking, trigger-tempered irrational deputy; small wonder the town council had clamored for his resignation.

He appeared formidable and confident when he descended the stairs to rejoin her. He didn't seat himself, just reached for her hand and held it while quietly confiding,

"It's okay with Pete. Sorry I can't say how long I'll be gone, but I'll be back, Hildy."

"You'll win no prize for guessing who'll be pining for you — and praying for you — till you do come back," she said softly. "It has to be rightaway?"

"Like to be on my way inside an hour," he muttered. "I still own a horse and saddle. All I have to do is change my clothes and pick up a few provisions. 'Be seeing you, Hildy."

"Come back to me healthy," she begged. "And with a smile on your face."

In his hotel room, Tyne changed to his riding clothes and, before venturing forth again, cleaned, oiled and loaded a Winchester and a Colt .45. The Colt was holstered and a filled shellbelt strapped on, after which he took up rifle, packroll and saddlebags and hurried to a store. From there, he carried his gear to the livery where his strawberry roan was stabled. He was saddled up and riding out of Beauvais fifty minutes after saying goodbye to Hildy Fitzgerald.

The morning was sunny but chilled by the lingering winter when Inez Durley first visited the line shack at Clear Creek. She had arrived early at Box Q, only to find that Marcie had left even earlier to call on another friend of hers, the daughter of the Circle Nine boss. As inept as ever, Inez hadn't thought to advise Marcie in advance.

"If she'd known," frowned Chloe Quiddon.

"My fault, Mrs Quiddon." Self-accusation was an Inez Durley characteristic. "Foolish of me to forget Marcie has other friends and not have sent word I was coming."

"Out riding all by yourself," Chloe noted.

"I so enjoy riding," enthused Inez, while Chloe admired her pinto filly. "And one thing Uncle Walter and I do agree on is . . ."

"Yes," nodded Chloe. "Sheriff Hallam and his deputies scared all the riff-raff out of Kimber County. It's safe nowadays for women to ride alone. Not that Marcie's riding alone, mind you. We take no chances. Luther'll stay with her all the way to Circle Nine and fetch her back."

All the better, Inez was thinking, as she rode through the hills. She could visit Marcie some other time and could now spend a longer period with the new hands of Clear Creek.

The new hands were out and about, flushing bunch-quitters back to graze when they sighted the young woman emerging from the hills to ford the creek.

"Don't spook," Stretch called good-humoredly. "She ain't the same female and it don't look like she's bein' chased."

Larry, closest to the creek, sat his mount and warily studied the rider in flowered bonnet, heavy shawl and broadcloth gown. Unlike the other female visitor, this one rode astride and, he conceded, sat the pinto well. Then he changed his mind. Halfway across, the pinto stumbled on a submerged rock, causing the rider to part company with her saddle. He thought this to be one of the dumbest mishaps he had ever witnessed. An easy fording till the horse stumbled. She might have stayed astride and in control of the filly had she not waved to Stretch. The splash, the sudden disappearance of the woman, irritated him, but did not alarm him. The creek was too shallow for her to drown. Well, provided she had savvy enough to raise her head above water.

She did that, rising, spluttering, wet bonnet askew. He called to her impatiently, while Stretch rode onto the scene to assist the pinto.

"Just wade out, lady, keep comin'."

Unaided, the filly made it to the south bank to toss a wet mane and swish a wet tail. Stretch dismounted and gallantly offered a hand.

"Lemme help, ma'am."

"Terribly clumsy of me," she panted. "Most embarrassing."

"You hurt?" demanded Larry.

"Only my dignity, Mister . . . ?" she smiled politely.

"Lawrence," he said. "This is Woodville, my partner."

"How do you do, gentlemen." The social niceties were observed while she stood dripping. "My name is Durley, Miss Inez Durley of Kimber City. I was, as you'll have guessed, enjoying one of my favorite pastimes and, really, Mildred is most reliable and well-trained . . ."

"Except she stumbled and dunked you," said Larry.

"My fault," she hastened to assure

him. "I wouldn't dream of blaming Mildred."

"Neither would I," he retorted. "Listen now, Miss Inez, you're gonna catch your death in them wet duds 'less you get yourself into the shack muy pronto and peel off. Don't worry about us. The shack's all yours for as long as you need it."

"How very k-k-kind."

"You can help yourself to a blanket."

"I'm m-most g-g-grateful . . ."

"Better hustle, Miss Inez."

"Allow me, Miss Inez." The very helpful Stretch unhitched and offered his lariat. "You can rig a line for hangin' your duds on."

"Throw some extra wood in the stove and the shack'll be warm enough," urged Larry. "Safer for you in there than out here in this cold wind."

She was still thanking them as she made her way to the shack. When the door closed behind her, the tall men traded frowns. Again, Stretch pointed out,

"Nobody chased her here. She was just out ridin'. Ain't gonna be no ruckus this time."

"Well . . . " shrugged Larry.

"Somethin' about Miss Inez got you fazed?" challenged Stretch.

"Can't put my finger on it, but there's somethin'," grouched Larry.

"What kinda somethin'?" demanded Stretch.

"She's clumsy," Larry said defensively. "Let's just say I'm leery of clumsy females."

It seemed a safe guess that the visitor's clothes would need time to dry, so the filly was led to the barn, offsaddled with the other animals and given a rubdown. The Texans then hunkered a short distance from the shack's door, their backs turned to it, and fished out their makings.

They were building smokes when the door opened. Inez called to them, but southern chivalry prevailed; they did not turn their heads.

"I have to wring out my garments,

otherwise they'd drip on your floor," she announced.

"Go right ahead, don't mind us," offered Larry.

Every item was wrung out, the bonnet and boots the only exceptions. The shack door was closed again. Larry glanced over his shoulder. Smoke was billowing from the chimney, sparks scattering, she had certainly built up the stove.

Their cigarettes were down to three-quarter-inch stubs when the door opened again.

"It's — all right to turn around," she assured them.

They rose and turned. Shrouded in a blanket, her hair in disarray, she was a comical sight right now; however they refrained from laughing.

"Best stay inside," Larry advised.

"Thank you, Mister Lawrence, yes, but ... "

"Somethin' else you need?" he asked.

"It's this blanket — and it's so hot inside," she said hesitantly. "Very rough, the blanket. If you'll forgive the indelicacy, it makes me itch."

"Plenty sun on the porch now, if you want to set." He nodded to a rocking chair.

"Thank you — you're so kind — but the itching . . ."

"Tell you what," he said. "Our other shirts're in there. We're some taller'n you so, long as you button it up, you'll be covered respectable."

"I'm so very much obliged. You're being so patient and — I'm afraid I'm a bother."

"No bother at all. Just help yourself."

When next she appeared, Stretch's shirt hung on her, its tails dangling about her ankles. She chose the rocker on which the sun shone and seated herself very carefully. Larry perched on the porchrail. Stretch sagged into the other rocker.

"Well — isn't this nice?" She smiled winsomely. "I do enjoy visiting people. But dear me — I'm more an intruder than a guest, aren't I?"

"It's okay," shrugged Larry.

"We don't mind, Miss Inez," mumbled Stretch. "Just so long as you ain't runnin' away from home and gettin' chased by your pa and a couple brothers hankerin' to beat up on us."

"Heavens, no," she frowned. "I'll be no problem, I promise. That was all terrible unfortunate, your little misunderstanding with Marcie's father."

"You know about it?" challenged Larry.

"She's a friend of mine," said Inez. "Really a very nice girl but — I must admit — rather impulsive. And please don't judge the Quiddons too harshly. They're fine people." She heaved a sigh. "Of course you wouldn't have heard, being all by yourself here in this isolated place. It was all for nothing, gentlemen. Ace Healey *was* a cheat. He was ordered by Sheriff Hallam to leave town. Which he has."

"Your folks'll be worryin' about you," suggested Stretch.

"Oh, no," she shrugged. "They know

I like to ride, so they don't expect me home at any special time. I should explain I live with an uncle and aunt in Kimber City. My parents are dead, you see. I help my aunt around the house and also work part-time for Mrs McEvoy, who owns a ladies' emporium."

"Nice town for a young lady, huh?" asked Stretch.

"Kimber City is as friendly a place as you could find," she said earnestly. "I do hope you won't think unkindly of our happy community because of that — that terrible violence at the Queen of Diamonds Saloon."

"How'd you know ... ?" began Larry.

"Mister Quiddon asked you," she said. "You told him and Marcie told me. I'm so sorry it happened. You seem such — uh — non-violent gentlemen."

"Well," said Larry. "There wouldn't have been no hassle if we hadn't got pushed into it."

"Meanwhile, we like it here," grinned

Stretch. "We're sure beholden to Milt Jacklin."

"Dear old Mister Jacklin, everybody admires him, Mrs Jacklin too," she smiled. "Did you meet their daughters?" They nodded. "More friends of mine, Sue, Genevieve and Justine."

"Either of them Quiddon boys courtin' you, Miss Inez?" asked Stretch. "Don't mean to be personal, mind. It's just my partner and me'd be plumb surprised if you wasn't spoke for."

"Such a gallant thing to say, so kind," she beamed. "Oh, you really are gentlemen, aren't you?"

"We try," grunted Larry. Remembering Marcie Quiddon, he felt entitled to add, "We try real hard."

"I don't think Newton and Luther give much thought to marriage," she said. "But, yes, there is an interested gentleman. Damien is chief cashier at the Merchants and Settlers Bank."

"Sounds like he'll do fine," remarked Stretch.

"I'm in no hurry," she said. Gazing

about, she asked, "Won't it be lonely for you here. And monotonous? Sue told me the men on line shack duty become cantankerous and fight among themselves."

"This place suits us fine," Larry assured her. "We like it quiet."

"Been partners a good long time," offered Stretch. "And we never get to fightin', leastways not each other, on accounta my buddy hits as hard as me."

"You're being so hospitable, I feel I should show my appreciation," she said. Another bright smile. "I have an idea. Let me make lunch. The stove's hot and it would be no trouble, and Aunt Clara would vouch for my cooking."

"Real friendly notion, Miss Inez," nodded Larry. "But don't cook for just us. Your duds won't be dry yet, so stay and eat."

The drifters could not find fault with the repast prepared by their unusual guest. They chose to eat on the porch. The breeze was not so chilly now and, inside the shack, decorated with the lady's dangling unmentionables, the atmosphere was somewhat steamy.

To Larry's relief, she did not barrage them with questions during that meal. Inquisitive women irked him almost as much as the clumsy ones, and the liars. After lunch, she retreated into the shack, felt her hanging garments and decided it was time to redon them. Stretch saddled the pinto filly and led it from the barn and, looking somewhat bedraggled, her wrecked bonnet perched precariously, she emerged to be farewelled. They asked if she knew her way back to town. She assured them she was familiar with every corner of the county and all the trails leading to the county seat.

"It's been so pleasant visiting with you," she said cheerily. "May I call again next time I'm riding?"

"You'd be plumb welcome, Miss Inez," grinned Stretch.

"Ride safe," urged Larry.

Stretch boosted her astride the pinto and accorded her a jerky bow. She rewarded him with a smile, waved to Larry and wheeled the filly to ride off to the southwest. Stretch returned to his rocker to build another cigarette.

"That was real sociable," he commented. "Just the same, runt, we weren't craving company."

"They told us nobody ever comes here," muttered Larry. "And I'd as soon nobody did."

"She's friendly enough and I'll allow she cooks good, but there's somethin' about her," frowned Stretch.

"A little squirrely you mean?" prodded Larry. "I noticed that too."

"Still and all, she ain't shifty like her friend Marcie," Stretch pointed out.

At this time, noon-camped en route to Deemsville on the Utah-Wyoming border, Jarvis Ames and his minions accounted for an austere meal and caught up on rest. It happened that Lafe Hartigan was squatting beside the Joad brothers and out of earshot of Ames, so Roy now gave in to curiosity.

"We all got our reasons for what we

hanker to do to them Texas hot shots," he said softly. "But I'm wonderin' about Ames. It ain't just on accounta his buddy Drood is it? Back at the spread, he turned mean when you talked of an older score. What was that all about?"

"Look, I'll tell you, but you gotta keep it under your hats," said Hartigan. "It's a secret thing with Jarv."

"We can keep a secret," shrugged Noah. "We're just curious is all."

"Happened about eight years back and Jarv's never forgot," confided Hartigan. "He hates Valentine's insides, gonna keep on hatin' till Valentine's down and dead. There was this purty woman ran a saloon in Lubock, Colorado. Jarv and me were there and so was Valentine and his partner. Jarv was strong for that woman, believe me. Hungered for her he did. Tried makin' it with her by buyin' presents for her, you know? She wasn't interested. Damned if she didn't laugh in his face. And then them Texans came sashayin' in to buy a drink and she gave 'em the glad eye — specially

Valentine — and told Jarv 'There's my idea of a *real* man. You ain't half the man Larry Valentine is, so don't bother me, mister.' Well, I'm tellin' you it was like she'd kicked Jarv where he lives. He took it bad and, ever since, he tried to forget her — but he can't get her out of his mind, her or Valentine."

"Man's a fool for lettin' a woman get to him that way," sneered Roy. "One woman's no better'n another."

"Now you know why Jarv craves to gun Valentine down," said Hartigan. "But now, if you're smart, forget I told you — and don't never talk of it to him."

"Think we'll find 'em in Deemsville?" demanded Noah.

"We'll make Deemsville before sundown," said Hartigan. "If they're still there, we'll find 'em — and take care of 'em. Like Clay says, it's gotta be done."

4

Greed and Treachery

IN pairs, the man-hunters drifted into the border town from west, north and south; a seven-man band, Ames had decided, could appear conspicuous and arouse curiosity, including that of Deemsville's lawmen.

The Joads were with Hartigan in the general store where further supplies were purchased. It was the elder brother who, glancing to a mirror behind the counter from where he was standing, spotted the open cashbox clearly reflected on the ledge under the counter. The storekeeper made change from the bill handed him by Hartigan and Roy Joad's avarice was skillfully masked; he had noted the contents of the cashbox. Later during their brief visit to this town, he confided his discovery to his brother, who grinned eagerly and remarked,

"Every little helps."

"It'll be dead easy," muttered Roy. "But now ain't the time, little brother. My guess is we'll nightcamp east a ways. That's when we'll make our move."

"Ames'll give us an argument," warned Noah. "He's bossin' this hunt."

"Leave all the talkin' to me," said Roy.

In a mid-town bar, Ames treated the barkeep to a drink and put his question. The barkeep was only too ready to brag of having pulled beer for the famous Lone Star Drifters.

"About two and a half weeks ago they were right here in Deemsville. Yes siree, mister, Larry and Stretch as big as life and friendly as you please. Couple real sociable gents, those fiddlefoots."

In another bar, Furth and Brandon talked to the stablehand of the barn in which Larry's sorrel and Stretch's pinto had been accommodated overnight. The stablehand recalled their departure.

"East from here."

"You sure?" prodded Brandon.

"Ain't as young as I used to be, but my memory don't fail me," shrugged the stablehand. "East they traveled."

Furth and Brandon sought Ames out to report the information they'd obtained and, fifteen minutes later, the seven were gone from Deemsville, five of them assuming they would never see this town again, two of them dead certain they would.

Ames' choice of a nightcamp was a box canyon some little distance north of the east-west trail. A fire was built and a meal prepared and cooked by Hartigan and Beavis. The hunters circled the fire, eating, speculating as to how far they would have to track their quarry.

"It doesn't matter," Ames declared. "We're all committed to this one purpose. How far we have to travel, how long it will take to run them to ground is unimportant — compared to the pleasure of being rid of them once and for all."

"I'll bet you're plannin' on gut-shootin' Valentine," said Beavis. "Like you gut-shot that over-the-hill badge-toter in Beauvais."

"Hey, we really cleaned up that day," grinned Brandon.

"It'd please me to see Valentine die slow," muttered Ames.

"Somethin' worth waitin' for," enthused Furth.

"Somethin' *I* can't wait for," drawled Roy Joad. He nudged his empty plate aside and drained his coffeecup. "I'm gonna have to head back to Deemsville. What d'you say, little brother? Wanta come along for the ride?"

"Might's well," shrugged Noah.

Ames frowned at them.

"What're you talking about?"

"Talkin' about ridin' back to Deemsville," Roy said casually. "Oughtn't take long. I figure we'll be back here by midnight."

"We've crossed the border," said Ames. "We're in Wyoming now and we'll push on east. There'll be no turning back for any of us. We travel together all the way, none of us separating from the party."

"Like I said, we'll be with you again when we break camp," said Roy. "Meanwhile, I gotta have a gunsmith check my iron. The firin' pin ain't right and, if you think I'm goin' up against them saddlebum heroes with a gun that could fail me, you got another think comin'."

"I noticed a gunsmithery in Deemsville," remarked Noah. "Chances are it won't take long to get it fixed."

"You should've had it seen to before we left town," chided Ames.

"Wasn't time," complained Roy. "We were there to find out about the sonsabitches we're after. Soon as Bob and Clay told you they'd been and gone, you said move out." Defiantly, he got to his feet; his brother followed suit. "You're bossin' this game, but that don't mean you can pin us down like you're Sergeant Ames and us a couple green troopers."

"Gotta be reasonable," wheedled Noah. "Where's the sense to Roy packin' a forty-five that's apt to fail him when it matters most?"

"When my life could be on the line," growled Roy.

"They got a point, Jarv," suggested Hartigan.

Ames scowled impatiently.

"All right," he nodded. "But get it done fast. Don't linger in Deemsville. Just get that weapon fixed and get out again."

The Joads ambled to the picket-line to ready their mounts. A few minutes later, they were quitting the canyon, making for the trail and chuckling triumphantly.

"Easy pickin's," the younger brother predicted,

"Another damn fool storekeeper," Roy Joad said contemptuously. "Just like the other two."

It was typical of their arrogance that, upon their return to Deemsville, they stopped by a saloon before heading for the general store of Nathan Elkins. After their third shot of whiskey, they decided they were ready for anything, invincible. From that saloon, they made their way to the alley running parallel with the main street on the east side. Their horses were left a short distance from the store's rear door.

Roy knocked, not loudly, but persistently. In pants and boots, his nightshirt tucked into his pants, Elkins lit a lamp in his kitchen and made the fatal mistake of unlocking and opening the door. A gun was shoved in his belly. He was forced clear of the threshold and the door reclosed.

"Not a yap outa you," leered Roy. "Not even a whisper."

His brother checked the storekeeper's pants pockets and found a ring of keys.

"Paydirt," he chuckled.

Roy Joad chuckled too, as he withdrew his Colt from Elkin's belly, uncocked it, raised it and struck. Elkins sagged to the floor.

"Fetch the lamp," ordered Roy.

They moved into the store, hunkered behind the counter and made short work of unlocking and opening the cashbox. The contents were stowed in Roy's pockets, after which they killed the lamp, returned to the kitchen, let themselves out and locked the door behind them. The keyring disappeared after Noah tossed it to a manure heap.

Unhurriedly they remounted. Why draw attention by quitting town at a gallop? They idled their horses down the alley and, by way of a narrower alley, reached the main street and crossed it slowly. Not until they were well and truly out of sight and sound of the township did they hustle their mounts to speed. They crossed the border some twenty minutes after midnight and, by 1 a.m., were offsaddling in the box canyon.

After breakfast two days later, the Texans donned chaps and saddled up for the routine chore of checking the herd and retrieving strays. It was then, just as they were about to mount, that the distant but ominous sound reached them. The wind was blowing from the north and the sound familiar to them. It wasn't repeated, but could not be disregarded.

"Maybe just one," frowned Larry.

"Uh huh," grunted Stretch. "Mountain cat — and hungry I bet."

"Yeah, well . . ." Larry fished out a coin. "We're here to make sure Milt's prime critters stay healthy — which they won't if a cougar comes raidin'. Call it. Heads you hunt the cat while I guard the herd. Tails I hunt and you ride guard."

The dime came down heads. Stretch unsheathed his rifle, levered a shell into the breech and got mounted.

"'Be seein' you, runt."

"Watch yourself," urged Larry. "Remember it's the cat should come up dead, not you."

"I'll keep that in mind," Stretch promised with a bland grin.

After his partner rode off toward the creek, Larry readied his own Winchester, resheathed it, swung astride and made for the herd. For an hour, he circled the sweet graze lazily, tallying, also keeping his ears cocked. Only two bunch-quitters. He tagged their tracks to the timber west and, without difficulty, flushed them out of there and ran them back to graze. He then sat his mount between the herd and the creek, rolled and lit a cigarette and, for another hour, listened for the bark of his partner's rifle. It would not be Stretch's first killer cat; he usually scored with one shot.

The wind had changed when the taller Texan finally glimpsed the marauding cougar. That brief glimpse warned him the beast had caught the scent of Milt's prime beeves and was moving south. Now the pursuit began, he hustling his pony through the hills toward the creek, the cougar breaking into a run. This wasn't going to be easy, he warned himself. To stop the killer this side of the creek, he would have to shoot from the saddle. He sighted the beast again and leveled his rifle and what followed convinced Larry once and for all that lightning can strike in the same place twice.

Watching the heights beyond the creek, Larry was distracted by another rider. Miss Inez Durley of Kimber City was visiting again, fording astride Mildred who, this time, picked her way with care. A different bonnet, different gown and shawl, but undoubtedly the same Inez happily waving to him. Then, when she was half-way across, the bark of Stretch's rifle was heard. He missed with his first shot, but every bullet has to end its flight somewhere, and this .44.40 slug went into the creek, after searing the rump of the pinto filly, which promptly loosed a shrill nicker and reared in agitation with the inevitable consequences for Inez. Larry shook his head in exasperation as she pitched into the water.

Stretch's rifle barked again as Larry rode to the creek. He scored a kill with that second shot, must have, because he appeared on the north bank a few moments later, just in time to see his partner capture the filly's rein and the other female rising to wade out. He gaped.

"Again?" he asked in wonderment.

Noting the burn-mark, Larry made to lead the filly to the shack. Inez reached the near bank, dripping, and began her all-my-fault routine.

"Dear me — most embarrassing — and so clumsy . . ."

"Do it, Inez," growled Larry. "Tag me to the shack . . ."

"I'll have to dry my . . ."

"Yep. Get out of them duds before you catch your death."

"And I'll need . . ."

"Extra wood in the stove. Help yourself to a shirt."

"And . . ."

"Wring 'em out and hang 'em. This

time you can use mine."

He tossed her his lariat and made for the shack, leading the still complaining filly. By the time she arrived, Stretch had forded and was approaching in urgent haste, and Larry emerged from the shack with right hand cupped.

"Poor Mildred . . ." she fretted.

"As good a soother as any," he said curtly. "Stretch's first slug burned her butt."

"But we're friends," she protested. He thought this a foolish statement. "Mister Woodville would never shoot at me!"

"He was huntin' a mountain cat," growled Larry. "Inside, Inez. Hustle!"

She trailed water up the steps and into the shack, while he gently applied lard to the smarting section of Mildred's rump. Almost at once, the filly responded. The quivering ceased. Stretch dismounted and, with trembling hands, began reloading his rifle.

"Holy Hannah!" he said shakily. "If

my first slug'd come a mite higher, I could've killed her!"

"You don't have to feel guilty," shrugged Larry. "It would've been an accident."

"Hell, runt . . . " groaned Stretch.

"Get that cat with your second shot?" Larry knew he had, but voiced the question to distract him from his shock.

"Only a little ways north of the creek," mumbled Stretch. "Big'un, amigo. Wind changed. He smelled the herd sure enough."

"Bueno," grunted Larry. "You did good. Now simmer down and quit your frettin'. I'll take care of the horses. You go rest yourself."

While he was offsaddling the animals in the barn, Stretch filled a rocker on the porch and rolled and lit a cigarette. Smoke and sparks rose from the chimney. Inez, shrouded in the taller Texan's other shirt, emerged burdened with her dripping garments and proceeded to wring them out. "Imposing on you again — this is really too bad," she accused herself. "And so embarrassing. You must let me . . ."

"Sure," sighed Stretch. "You can fix lunch."

His chores finished, Larry reappeared. The apologies began again.

"I'm most *terribly* sorry, Mister Lawrence. What must you think of me?"

"Don't ask," he advised. "Just wring 'em out, hang 'em and stay warm in there."

When she was back inside and draping her clothing on the makeshift line, he fished out his makings and squatted on the edge of the porch.

"I could've killed her," fretted Stretch.

"Forget it," said Larry.

"That would've been a helluva sad thing," muttered Stretch. "I mean, we're gettin' used to her. We'd miss her."

"Speak for your own doggone self," scowled Larry.

They sat smoking, busy with their own thoughts, until Inez came out to join them, helping herself to the other rocker and announcing,

"My clothes are all hung and lunch is cooking."

"Yeah, fine," said Larry.

"Well, isn't this nice?" She demurely smoothed the tails of Stretch's shirt about her bare ankles. "Here we are again — and just like the last time."

"Been visitin' Box Q," guessed Larry. "On your way home, said to yourself why don't I stop by Clear Creek again? So you came through the hills and fell in the creek again."

"It's really *too* embarrassing," she murmured. "What must you think of me?"

"You asked that before," said Larry. "I'm still workin' on it."

"Poor Mildred," she frowned. "How frightening for her."

"She'll be fine, Miss Inez," Stretch hastened to assure her. "Better her than you. Wasn't no trouble for my partner to rub a little lard on — uh — on where she got bullet-burned, but if it'd been you, he couldn't — I mean — no that *ain't* what I mean!" In anguish, he began rephrasing the statement. "It's one thing to rub lard on a horse's butt, but it wouldn't be polite to . . . !"

"It's gettin' worse," Larry dryly warned. "Better leave it be."

"So peaceful here," remarked Inez.

"Used to be," growled Larry, glancing northward.

Riders were fording the creek, three cowhands who hustled their mounts to the near bank and, after a casual appraisal of the J Bar beeves, idled toward the shack. Inez winced uneasily while, wary-eyed, the Texans read the brands. Box Q. The Quiddon hands reined up, noted her unconventional garb and addressed the drifters.

"Tracked strays into the hills," one of them drawled. "Heard shootin', so got curious."

"Knew Inez come visitin' the spread," said another. "Figured we oughta check — 'case she bought trouble on her way home?"

"My partner did the shootin'," Larry said calmly.

"Uh huh," nodded the third waddy. "We just now rid past a dead cougar." He leered at Inez." "Right purty get-up, Inez."

"Well now," grinned the first man. "Ain't this cosy?"

The second man sniffed inquisitively.

"Somethin' smells good," he remarked to Larry. "She comes by to fix supper too — stays for breakfast?"

"Mind your mouth," growled Larry.

"Don't push it, feller," the man retorted. "Try mixin' it with us and you'll find we're some rougher'n old Enoch and his boys."

"What's under the shirt, Inez?" challenged the first man.

"Hey, Curly, I bet *these* jaspers've seen what's under the shirt," chuckled the third one.

That did it for Larry, for Stretch also. They were suddenly off the porch and the last taunter was suddenly off his horse; Larry wrenched his boot from stirrup, heaved mightily and forced him over the animal's back to hit ground with a resounding thud. The other two promptly swung down and lashed out at the Texans while Inez, rising and moving to the edge of the porch, began an explanation.

"It's all quite innocent really — the reason you find me en deshabille..." She flinched as a gasping Box Q man reeled from Stretch's haymaker and crashed to the steps. "En deshabille — that's French — you may not be familiar with the expression. It means..."

Her eager explanation continued, the struggling scrappers oblivious to her, bent only on a fast exchange of blows, she appealing to them from the porch. Larry dodged a kick, scored with a right to the jaw and drove his assailant against a pony which pranced clear of him and whinnied a protest. Then all three animals were milling and dust rising and the Texans still under attack, striking out with relish and vigor, wreaking havoc.

"Couldn't we — *discuss* this misunderstanding . . . ?" Inez pleaded, as a bloody-mouthed waddy hit the ground shoulders-first. "This violence is so unnecessary!"

A cursing cowpoke made the serious error of charging Stretch head-down with the obvious intention of butting him in the midriff. Stretch let him get close enough and, with devastating timing, brought his knee up. The man's face made jarring impact with it and he hurtled backward, while the last aggressor landed a blow to the side of Larry's head, only to suffer painful retaliation. Larry lurched, righted himself and slammed a left to the ribs, following that with a swinging right to the jaw; that one didn't crumple, but went down stiffly, like a felled pine.

" . . . and Mildred was startled . . . " Inez was chattering on earnestly. "She didn't mean to throw me — she's really a very well-behaved animal — but then

I was in the creek again and . . ."

"Forget it, Inez," panted Larry. "They can't hear you."

The Texans were still upright, the losers horizontal and staying that way, till Larry grasped a fistful of hair and hauled one to a kneeling position. Stretch hauled another to his feet by a coat-collar.

"Now let's hear it," he said threateningly. "C'mon! The lady's waitin'!"

"Sorry, Inez," the man groaned.

"Didn't mean nothin'," mumbled the man grasped by Larry.

The still prone one rolled over, sighed heavily and added his apology.

"Just joshin' you, Inez."

"Now climb on them critters and get the hell out of here," ordered Larry. "I don't want to see you big-mouths again, savvy?"

To the accompaniment of much wincing and gasping, three soreheaded waddies struggled back into their saddles and, very slowly, turned their mounts toward the creek. The Texans followed them on foot, waited for them to ford and disappear into the hills, then flopped by the bank to dunk their heads. They returned to the shack streaming water and in ill humor.

"Not that you ain't welcome, Inez," Larry said irascibly. "But now maybe you understand why you oughtn't come visit us."

"*We* know you're a lady," Stretch pointed out. "And *you* know you're a lady."

"But it's kind of important every other hombre should know it," growled Larry. "Three dumb cowhands come by, see you rigged in nothin' but a man's shirt — what're they gonna think?"

"How poignant," she sighed. "It's all so innocent. I seem to be prone to foolish accidents — and you've been so patient, Mister Lawrence." She retreated into the excessive humidity of the shack, came out again and made to dab at her sweating brow with the tail of the shirt, but thought better of it in the nick of time and blushed profusely. Summoning up an encouraging smile, she reseated herself and murmured, "Never mind. Lunch will soon be ready."

They flopped again, still disgruntled.

"Nobody comes to Clear Creek, Milt said," grouched Stretch. "Well, we know somethin' he don't know, right?"

"You said it," nodded Larry.

"I've displeased you," Inez said contritely. "Oh, this is really *too* bad. You've both been so kind to me, and I've repaid your kindness by disrupting your tranquility."

"By — doin' what?" blinked Stretch.

"Makin' a hash of our peace and quiet," Larry translated.

"How can you ever forgive me?" she said brokenly.

"Don't blubber," chided Larry.

"Did those foolish cowboys hurt you?" she asked.

"You weren't payin' attention — just talkin'," he said. "*They* got hurt."

"And then some," mumbled Stretch.

"I did notice — how energetically you fought them," she said. "You were so active and terribly aggressive. And it's really sad."

"What d'you mean sad?" frowned Larry.

"How to explain my feelings?" she mused. "You were aggressive, but in a dogged way, much as though you had resigned yourselves to it. I shouldn't ask questions of such gracious hosts, it would be a breach of etiquette, but ..."

"Go ahead," he shrugged. "Ask."

"That terrible disturbance I heard of, at the saloon in Kimber City, and your disagreement with Mister Quiddon and his sons, and now this," she murmured. "I don't mean to offend, but it does seem to me — you're accustomed to such violent activity."

The Texans traded sober glances. Stretch shrugged fatalistically and admitted,

"We've gotten into a hassle or two a time or two."

"We move around a lot," Larry told their guest. "Restless, you know? And we end up havin' to protect ourselves 'most every place we go."

"But it don't pleasure us none," muttered Stretch. "Shucks, Miss Inez, if we never had to bust another jaw or stop a faceful of fist, we'd like that fine. It's what we always wanted."

"How truly sad that is," she commented.

"We try not to complain of it," said Larry. "Not too much anyway."

"Complainin' ain't manly," remarked Stretch. "And it's liable to irk folks."

Abruptly, Larry changed the subject. Testing the air with a wet fingertip, he casually predicted.

"Gonna be an early spring, like Milt and Pike said."

"Wind's still cold, but we've known colder," said Stretch. "Herd's lookin' good, huh runt?"

"Milt's special critters," mused Larry.

"The mountain lion Mister Woodville had to shoot, would it have attacked me, do you think?" asked Inez. "Or poor Mildred?"

"Hungry cat'll go for beef when he catches scent of it," said Larry. "You were safe enough, till his first slug burned Mildred's butt."

"I hope you're partial to pork chops," she said, rising. "I took the liberty of investigating the cellar. Heavens, it's so *chilly* down there."

As on her last visit, they lunched on the porch, Stretch eating with relish, Larry still pondering the enigma of the so ladylike but so inept Miss Durley of Kimber City. Just what kind of woman was she anyway? Though not disliking her, he was irritated, and not just because of her clumsiness. There was something else, something he could not define.

By the time the meal ended, her clothes were dry. She dressed in the shack while Larry readied the pinto filly and Stretch visited the three-hole privy out back. She was, for obvious reasons, as bedraggled as on her first visit when she emerged to be helped astride her mount. Another bonnet ruined. Another gown wrinkled, creased in the wrong places.

She thanked them again before riding off. As well, she expressed the hope there would be no further disruptions of the peace they craved in this isolated place. They assured her she was voicing their own hopes, urged her ride carefully and, even before she was out of sight, opened the shack's only window and swung the door wide as a counter to the lingering heat radiating from the stove. Most of that afternoon they spent outdoors gathering firewood; in two visits, the lady from Kimber City had depleted their supply. They also got in a little fishing. No success, but a relaxing diversion.

By sundown, their fears were easing. There had been too much action of a violent nature at their hideaway haven, but now they assured themselves this had been an unfortunate coincidence. The remainder of their stint at Clear Creek would be tranquil — they hoped.

For the second time, Inez Durley was returning to her hometown looking less presentable than on her departure. As on that other occasion, she strove to avoid Main Street, surrendering the filly to a stablehand at the rear, not the street door of the barn a block from the Courier office. To get home, she had to cross Main. She did so hurriedly and, she hoped, unobtrusively, but was observed by a dozen or so curious locals.

Reaching the alley behind the double-storey that was home and office of the Kinstrys, she moved to the rear door, opened it quietly and entered the kitchen to be confronted by her aunt. She froze. Clara, rallying bravely, nodded and remarked,

"You need to change your clothes, dear. To put it mildly."

"I do feel somewhat disheveled," Inez admitted.

"I can understand why," said Clara.

To get to the stairs leading up to the living quarters, Inez had to move through the office. She did so without winning even a casual glance from the brothers Kinstry, both absorbed in their chores.

In her bedroom, after she had changed to a fresh gown and was brushing her hair, her aunt knocked and entered. Seating herself, Clara said her piece as diplomatically as she was able.

"Now, Inez dear, you must realize by now that we Kinstrys have grown very fond of you, though you could be excused for believing your Uncle Walt regards you as a pest. That's just his way, you understand. He can be a less than patient man, but he means well and is properly concerned for your welfare and, of course, your future."

"I do understand, Aunt Clara," Inez said warmly. "And I do appreciate your giving me a home."

"Our bounden duty," said Clara. "You're the only child of my dear sister, God rest her soul, and now I think of you as one of my own. Also, Inez, I feel a responsibility toward you. You're of age now and seem — well — steady enough — but you must understand I'm deeply concerned for your moral welfare, your reputation as a respectable young lady of our community." She raised a hand placatingly. "I'm not suggesting anything, dear. However, I could not fail to notice this is the second time you've come home from a long ride with your hair untidy and your clothes rumpled." Inez smiled reassuringly, discarded her brush and went to pains to set her aunt's mind at ease. She was frank, but not completely. Her two mishaps at Clear Creek were accurately described, but no mention made of her very special project, an in-depth critical analysis of the character and personality traits of the line shack's current occupants. Much relieved, Clara went downstairs to repeat this explanation to her husband.

Kinstry deigned to stop pounding his typewriter long enough to give her a hearing. He digested it all, while his brother eavesdropped from his position at the press, grinning inwardly.

"Naturally she had to dry her clothes," Clara stressed. "This time of year, Walt, heaven help us, she could've taken pneumonia. But it was all quite respectable. The two J Bar hands simply turned the shack over to her and stayed outside."

"Well, Milt Jacklin doesn't hire trail-trash," he shrugged. "No danger they'd take liberties."

"As a gesture of her appreciation, she cooked a meal for them," said Clara.

"Very nice," he nodded. "I believe it, so *you* might as well believe it. We're speaking of your niece, don't forget, so it's entirely credible. Who else do you know who could suffer the same dumb mishap twice — in the same place — in the same way?"

"Only Inez," she sighed.

"Right," said Kinstry. "Only Inez. One of a kind, and a calamity in petticoats."

Brad Tyne, meanwhile, had visited Hallsburg and was destined to reach the border town of Deemsville two and a half days after Inez Durley's second unscheduled bath in Clear Creek.

5

Lone Hunter

WHILE headed for Deemsville, the ex-deputy marshal of Beauvais nursed the hope he would pick up another lead as to the whereabouts of his quarry. He kept the strawberry roan to a steady pace, but spelled it as often as he deemed wise, being reluctant to overtire an animal serving him so well.

It was noon when he sighted the border town and, when he idled his mount into its main street, he noted it was no bigger than his hometown. Certain buildings, a hotel, a store or two, were similar; he was reminded of Beauvais and, inevitably, of a loyal woman, shrewd-eyed and auburn-haired, who cared for him and made no demands on him. He remembered Hildy

Fitzgerald with affection, but only for a few moments. Better to concentrate on his mission of vengeance, he warned himself. Until it was over and done with, he would be no use to Hildy nor any other woman, nor to himself.

The hitch-rail to which he tied the roan was in shade and a trough within reach. Close by was the Cinch Strap Saloon, which seemed a quiet place; he could hear conversation, but no raucous laughter, no voices raised. When the roan's thirst was slaked, he slipped its rein and led it to the nearest livery stable. The hand on duty offsaddled the animal.

"Feed and rubdown?"

"Right," nodded Tyne. "He's earned it."

Returning to the Cinch Strap, he made for the bar, ordered beer and built a sandwich from the counter fare. He then drew the barkeep into conversation, leading off by remarking the town seemed uncommonly quiet.

"Folk still thinkin' of the funeral,"

muttered the barkeep. "A killin' here some days back. You know how it goes, mister. People don't know how bad they'll miss a man till after he's cut down in his prime. Everybody knew him. He didn't run the only general store in town, but he was part of the community, one of us."

"Murdered," frowned Tyne.

"Right in his own kitchen, his skull stove in," said the barkeep. "Lived by himself, so it was daylight before he was found. Store didn't open on time. One of Mosely's deputies forced the rear door and there was Nate Elkins."

"Anything missing?" demanded Tyne.

"About a hundred and twenty dollars, I hear tell." The barkeep grimaced in disgust. "They found his cashbox open and empty. He'd have banked that money next mornin'."

Tyne accounted for two sandwiches and a refill of beer, dropped money on the bar and asked if Sheriff Mosely might be found in his office. Overhearing the question, another drinker remarked the sheriff usually had his lunch delivered from a nearby cafe.

"Real cool feller, Bart Mosely," he told Tyne. "But he's sure partial to hot grub. The chili from that Mex place'd blister my tongue. Mosely's welcome to it."

The stocky, heavy-featured sheriff of Deems County had finished his lunch by the time Tyne walked in on him. He swigged coffee, gave his visitor a cigar and listened to his questions. Before offering answers, he studied Tyne thoughtfully and asked,

"You kin of the late Jacob Tyne?"

"His son," nodded Tyne.

"We weren't close acquainted, but I heard of him often," said Moseley. "Rough way for him to go."

"Couldn't have been rougher," Tyne said grimly. "Look, I know word gets around. You've probably heard I fell apart after my parents' deaths. I'm not a deputy any more, but not a drunk either. And maybe I'm not too far behind the man who gunned my father down."

"All right, you asked about strangers in town about the time Elkins was killed," said Mosely. "Seems there were a half-dozen."

"So there could have been seven," opined Tyne. "Any of 'em familiar to you?"

"The Joad brothers, Roy and Noah," Mosely said bluntly. "I got pictures in my files, but no warrants. Yeah, they were here — twice."

"Left town, then came back?" prodded Tyne.

"One of my deputies recognized 'em the second time they rode out," said Mosely. "They didn't seem in a hurry, so he wasn't leery of 'em — until next morning."

"Five'll get you ten the Joads butchered the storekeeper," declared Tyne.

"I had the same idea," nodded Moseley. "Two other storekeepers got theirs the same way. The Joads were around, but nobody could prove anything."

"You tried to head 'em off, but they had too long a start," guessed Tyne.

"Tracked 'em to the border before I turned back," said Mosely. "But, before I deputed a posse, I wired the law authorities of a lot of towns in the West Wyoming territory so there'll be many a peace officer keeping a sharp eye out for the Joads. Keep your fingers crossed. They might get lucky."

"Still moving east," reflected Tyne. He finally got around to lighting his cigar. "Plain enough the whole gang didn't come here just to rob and kill a storekeeper. Deemsville wasn't Jarvis Ames's destination. I'll stay after him — but I wish I knew where he's headed and why."

"Ames, huh?" frowned Mosely. "Could mean another bank job."

"Meanwhile, they only stopped by here for supplies," Tyne surmised. "My hunch is the robbery was the Joads' own idea."

"For supplies and information," offered Mosely. "I talked to quite a few barkeeps and stablehands after I brought my posse back. Seems those strangers asked a lot of questions about the same two fiddlefoots — meaning Valentine and Emerson. I don't have to ask if you've heard of *them*. You used to be a lawman."

"Those Texans, the drifters?" challenged Tyne.

"The Joad boys and the bunch they're traveling with seemed mighty interested," said Mosely.

"They ever been here, Valentine and his sidekick?" asked Tyne.

"A little while back," said Mosely. "Didn't hang around long nor start any trouble, so I didn't even look 'em up." He grinned wryly. "I don't need the kind of aggravation they can cause, so my men had their orders. Hands off until they step out of line. Well, they kept their noses clean in Deemsville, never once stepped out of line, so that was that. They traveled on and

I forgot about 'em — till I found out the strangers were asking questions."

Tyne worked his cigar to the side of his mouth, half-closed his eyes and said softly,

"I wonder which direction *they* rode."

"Wonder no more," said Mosely. "I'm the one can tell you, because I saw 'em leave. They made for the Wyoming line."

"Well, well, well," said Tyne.

"Think it could mean something?" prodded Mosely.

"It's a switch," said Tyne. "Badmen are more inclined to ride clear of those trouble-shooters than to bird-dog 'em. But, if Ames has his reasons, it's a possibility I guess." He wrinkled his brow. "Valentine and Emerson pushing east into Wyoming, seven hard cases trailing 'em. Interesting."

"Anything else I can tell you?" asked Mosely.

"I'd be obliged if you'd steer me to a store that doesn't overcharge on staples," said Tyne. "I'm not toting a big bankroll, just enough for traveling expenses."

"Packham's on South Bain Street," offered Mosely. As Tyne rose to leave, "No proof, huh Tyne?" he challenged. "If Ames is still riding free, there couldn't have been any evidence against him."

"No proof, but no doubt in my mind," Tyne assured him. "He was well-known to me long before the bank raid in Beauvais. I'd talked to other lawmen and memorized all the descriptions. He moves in a certain way, a slight swagger they all said, and he favors a Smith and Wesson forty-four holstered to his left side, the butt reversed for a cross-draw."

"Not much to go on," suggested Mosely. "S and Ws are as plentiful as Colts and Remingtons. And you'll see many a handgun packed leftside by a righthanded man."

"Ames is my man," declared Tyne. "I'm determined he'll pay dearly for my father's death, but I'm not apt to go haywire, Mosely. If I can take him alive, I'll turn him over to the nearest law authority."

"And, if that S and W's in his hand when you find him . . . " began Mosely.

"It'll be Ames or me," vowed Tyne.

An hour later he was gone from Deemsville, taking the trail that would put him in Wyoming Territory in less than forty-eight hours.

Winter's chill was lingering the day Ames and his minions separated a mile from Strome's Ford on the Green River. The routine devised by the boss-hunter was followed again, he entering the river town from the south with Hartigan and Furth, Beavis and Brandon circling to move in from the north, the Joad brothers making for the main stem from the west.

It was 2 p.m. when one of the Ford's two law officers, Deputy Marshal Kell Raddick, located his boss in a barber shop. Burley Mat Brill was rising from the chair freshly shorn, the barber brushing him down.

"The Joad brothers," Raddick said tensely.

Brill frowned at him, paid the barber and reached for his hat and gunbelt.

"You sure?"

"Damn sure," growled Raddick. "Hell, Mat, remember the wire from Deemsville?"

"You don't have to remind me," muttered Brill. "Where'd you see 'em?"

"Cowley's Bar," said Raddick. "Right there at the bar counter brazen as all get-out — those bastards."

"All right," nodded Brill. "I want those two unarmed in my office and answering questions, and fast."

"If I was you, Marshal, I'd ... " began the barber.

"The day you trade your scissors and razors for a badge and a six-gun, you can tell me what you'd do," Brill curtly rebuffed him. "Meanwhile, *I* know what I'm gonna do."

"Don't forget there's a back door at Cowley's," urged the barber, as the lawmen moved out.

"As if I'd forget Cowley's back door," Brill said impatiently.

"We move in slow and easy, huh?" suggested Raddick.

"Right," nodded Brill. "You from the front, me through the back door. Just belly up to the bar like you're about to order a drink, then prod your man with your iron and disarm him and, by the time you're doing that, I'll have the drop on the other one."

"But we take 'em out the street door?" grinned Raddick.

"Bet your life we do," chuckled Brill. "We're gonna march'em to the town jail right along Main Street for the whole town to see — and then maybe Clem Adams'll quit bragging of how the town council ought to fire me and give him my badge, that damn blowhard."

"This'll shut Adam's mouth," enthused Raddick.

The apprehension of the Joad brothers

was achieved quietly and without bloodshed. They were still at the bar, when Brill entered by way of the rear doorway, his deputy simultaneously moving in from the street. Casually, Raddick advanced to the bar to position himself at Roy Joad's left. Just as casually, Brill moved along to stand beside the young brother. Deftly, he got his left hand to Noah's gunbutt. The holster was empty, Brill's too, and his cocked .45 nudging Noah's ribs before the elder brother began reacting.

"I wouldn't, Joad," growled Raddick, the muzzle of his gun prodding his belly. "Keep your paws on the bar." He disarmed Roy, then nodded to Brill. "Okay, Mat."

"What the hell . . . ?" began Roy.

"Taking you boys in for questioning," announced Brill, while the barkeep gawked and the other drinkers edged away, "No rash moves now. We got the drop on you."

"And this ain't Deemsville," sneered Raddick.

"Our name ain't Joad and we've never been in Deemsville," protested Noah.

"Never even heard of Deemsville," complained Roy.

"The hell you haven't," jibed Raddick. "Ready, Mat?"

"Ready," nodded Brill. "Let's go, boys. Turn left when you've untied your horses, then lead 'em downtown and don't forget — not for one moment — we'll be right behind you. Try making a break and you're customers of the Strome's Ford undertaker."

"And you'd better believe it," Raddick said threateningly.

What Bob Furth saw from the opposite sidewalk a few moments later triggered prompt and decisive counter-action. He alerted Brandon and, when the local lawmen and their prisoners were still fifty yards from the town jail, Ames had been informed and was issuing orders; he was furious, but thinking clearly. The horses were collected and taken to the alley behind the jailhouse by Hartigan and Beavis.

No sooner had the door of the marshal's office closed behind the Joads and their captors than Brandon was untying their horses and leading them around to the rear of the building. Hartigan and Beavis took charge of them, after which Brandon returned to the street to join Ames and Furth.

The three climbed the steps to the porch, moved to the door, opened it and entered just as Raddick was about to hustle the prisoners into the cellblock.

"No questions, and don't raise your voices," muttered Ames, his gun out and leveled at the startled Brill.

"And keep your paws clear of your hardware," growled Furth.

Brandon closed and locked the street-door and lowered the shade on the front window. Bug-eyed, Brill and his deputy submitted to the indignity of being disarmed and gagged with their own kerchiefs. They were then forced to put their hands behind their backs; Furth secured their wrists with their own manacles while Ames helped himself to a keyring. The Joads retrieved and holstered their Colts.

Into the jailhouse, empty at this time, they hustled the lawmen. Ames found the key to a cell and unlocked it. Roughly they shoved Brill and Raddick into the cell. The door was shut and re-locked and then they were making for the door at the rear end of the passage.

At his third attempt, Ames found the right key. As he turned it in the lock, he cautioned his companions.

"No hustling. We just move out, get mounted and proceed slowly to the next side street south. Then we swing east again and, if our luck holds, we'll be across the river and far clear of this town before anybody starts wondering what became of those knucklehead lawmen."

"Real slick," Roy Joad remarked with an approving grin.

He loosed a gasp; Ames had rammed an elbow into his ribs, savagely.

"Not another word out of you!" Ames grimly chided. "You won't talk till I'm ready to hear your explanation and, by thunder, I'll want the truth!"

He opened the door. They moved out to their horses. Already mounted, Hartigan and Beavis were darting wary glances along the rear alley. The others swung astride and, with Ames leading, the seven idled their animals south to the next side street, then eastward. A short time later they were crossing the bridge spanning the Green, still maintaining an easy pace. No man sank spur until the river was a considerable distance behind.

The horses were winded by the time Ames finally called a halt. They were in high country now and had veered north from the trail to make for and ascend the near slope of a ridge to its timbered spine. Reaching it, they reined up and dismounted at Ames's command and, without waiting to be told, Hartigan and Beavis unsheathed rifles and chose lookout positions. They stared away toward the trail, while Ames confronted the Joads and began his interrogation.

"You weren't picked up for no reason," he muttered. "Nothing like this happened in the other towns we've passed through. You were recognized and seized in Strome's Ford and I want to know why."

"That fool marshal made a dumb mistake," shrugged Noah.

He raised a hand, but not fast enough. Ames's fist exploded in his face. He grunted, reeled backward and flopped on his backside and, with a snarled oath, his brother made to fill his hand. In a flash, Ames's Smith & Wesson was out and aimed at his head.

"Clay," said Ames.

"Now boys," Brandon drawled, relieving Roy of his gun, bending to take the younger brother's. "That was stupid. You oughta know better."

"I won't be lied to — understand?" Ames raged at Roy.

"Damn you, Ames, I ain't gonna forget this," scowled Roy.

"Remember this too!" retorted Ames.

His left hand swung, the back of it striking the elder brother's face with such force that he reeled off-balance. "Now *tell* me, you idiot! I want to know why ... " He paused, eyes gleaming. "Wait a minute! *Deemsville*! Against my better judgement, I let you fools return to Deemsville! That's where it happened?"

"You didn't need no gunsmith," accused Furth.

"*I'll* ask the questions," chided Ames.

Roy drew a sleeve across his mouth, glowered at him and said defiantly,

"Us Joads don't pass up a chance at easy money. We got a mite richer in Deemsville, took a storekeeper for every dollar in his cashbox."

"I might've guessed!" breathed Ames. "You lame-brained, dollar-greedy jackasses, every day brings us closer to Valentine and Emerson and settling our score with them! That's supposed to be our common goal — nothing else! Plain enough what happened. You were recognized in Deemsville and the local law must've spread the word by telegraph. So those Strome's Ford lawmen were *waiting* for you."

"Real dumb, boys," chided Brandon. "It was just our luck we broke you outa that jail without a fight."

"We could've found ourselves up against the whole damn town!" fumed Ames. "Because of you, some of us could still be in Strome's Ford — awaiting burial! Was that worth a handful of dollars from a Deemsville storekeeper's cashbox?"

"We played it real careful," mumbled Noah, picking himself up. "How'd we know they caught onto us?"

He recoiled in fear, seeing death in Ames's eyes and the muzzle of the Smith & Wesson now pointed at his belly. For a tense moment, it seemed both brothers were doomed. Then Furth said quietly,

"They're fast and tricky, the bastards we're after, Jarv. I'm bettin' it'll take all seven of us to put 'em down. So we can still use these hot shots."

A shudder wracked Ames's frame. He

glared balefully at the brothers.

"I'll say this just one more time," he muttered. "We're all in this together. It's a blood pact, all of us craving vengeance for kin or friends. We have two targets, Valentine and Emerson. Nothing else matters until we've done what we started out to do. When it's over, we can think about banks, stagecoaches and well-heeled merchants with full cashboxes. When it's over — not before. From here on, we stay together. I want to know where you Joads are every hour of the day or night and — this I promise — one more act of disobedience will be your last. I'll kill you both. Is that clear enough?"

The brothers traded glances. Roy shrugged impatiently and complained,

"It was just we were short of cash. If we'd guessed you'd go off half-cocked, we wouldn't have done it."

"You didn't have to get so all-fired mad at us," whined Noah.

"I asked you a question!" snarled Ames.

"Yeah, yeah, it's clear enough," nodded Roy. "Let up on us, damn it. We'll stay in line from here on."

Cold-eyed, in control of himself again, Ames holstered his pistol.

"Return their sidearms," he told Brandon.

Brandon did that. The brothers holstered their weapons and followed Ames, Brandon and Furth to where Hartigan and Beavis squatted by the horses with their eyes turned toward the trail.

"No more towns for us, huh Jarv?" frowned Hartigan. "Deemsville sheriff likely wired every tin star of West Wyomin'."

"It'll be a job for just one man," decided Ames. "One I can depend on to stay clear of inquisitive lawmen, gather the information we need and get back to us without a posse on his tail. Your chore, Bob. You can pass for a drifting ranch-hand and you know better than to make yourself conspicuous. The rest of us will camp somewhere in the region, somewhere off the beaten trails. Any supplies we need, you'll have to fetch them — along with whatever you can learn about the Texans."

"Anybody hear word of 'em at Strome's Ford?" asked Beavis.

"Me," said Brandon. "They passed through a while back. I talked to a gabby blacksmith. Seems Valentine's horse was near throwin' a shoe. And another citizen remembered 'em."

"They're still headed east," guessed Ames.

"East," nodded Brandon.

"Looks quiet," Hartigan remarked, staring westward. "It was just a two-bit river town, Jarv, with a town marshal and one deputy. Don't seem like we'll have a posse snappin' at our heels."

"No," agreed Ames. "But thanks to the Joads, a lot of lawmen are suddenly leery of strangers. The Ford is probably part of a county and the next sizeable town we reach could be the county seat."

"Which means there'll be a sheriff

and at least two deputies," said Beavis.

"*This* stranger'll tread wary," promised Furth.

"We'll spell the horses a few more minutes," said Ames. "Then we'll move on and, between now and sundown, we'll have to keep our eyes peeled for a nightcamp, somewhere there's shelter and good cover, a good defense position. Have to be on the alert for search parties from now on. Two men standing guard at every camp. We'll make it three-hour shifts so we'll all get as much sleep as we need."

"I'm feelin' lucky," announced Brandon. "Got this notion it won't be much longer, couple weeks at most." He chuckled harshly. "Helluva thing it's gonna be — all seven of us pumpin' lead into them heroes."

"A pleasure to be savored," Ames said with unholy fervor.

It was near sundown of that day when one of the more influential citizens of Strome's Ford, banker Virgil

Hardesty, rapped in vain at the town marshal's office door. He was still on the porch, wondering where he could find Brill, when a brawny local of his acquaintance climbed the steps to greet him. Clem Adams always accorded Hardesty respect; his livery stable had been established with the aid of a loan authorized by Hardesty in his capacity as manager of the Ford Trust.

"Howdy there, Mister Hardesty. Any way I can help?"

"Not unless you can tell me where to find Marshal Brill," said Hardesty. "He wasn't at any of his usual haunts and his office is locked. I couldn't find the deputy either."

"You wouldn't have any trouble findin' *me*, sir," Adams warmly assured him. "If *I* was marshal."

"Adams, I don't need to be reminded of your ambition to replace Brill," frowned Hardesty.

"Said it before and I'll say it again," declared Adams. "I near paid off my loan, the stable's doin' fine and I got

Pat Kellerby runnin' it for me — so I'm available."

"And you'd be a better marshal than Brill," Hardesty said impatiently.

"Got important business with him, have you?" prodded Adams.

"I hope he'll consider it important," said Hardesty, rapping at the door again. "There were strangers in town this afternoon. I didn't like their looks and one of them seemed very interested in the bank. He kept hanging around."

"That don't sound good," growled Adams. "If I'd known about it, I'd have braced him and made him explain himself."

"I want Brill to keep the bank under surveillance tonight, just in case," said Hardesty. "Now where the devil could he be?"

"Keep on knockin', Mister Hardesty," urged Adams. "I'll check the rear door." He was moving along the side alley to the back of the jailhouse when the muffled sound reached him. He jerked to a halt under a barred window, ears cocked, and heard it again. Not a groan, but an indignant, desperate voice striving to make itself heard, and with difficulty. Doubling back to the front porch, he informed the banker, "I heard somethin' sounds plenty suspicious to me. Stand aside, Mister Hardesty. I'm gonna bust the door in."

"Break the door down?" blinked Hardesty.

Frank Ball came by at this point and, his curiosity aroused, climbed to the porch to trade friendly greetings with Hardesty and ask questions. Being mayor of Strome's Ford, owner of a hotel, a saloon and a haberdashery store, he considered himself as important a citizen as his friend the banker.

"You're looking fretful, Virg," he observed. "Some kind of trouble here?"

"Brill and his deputy are missing and Adams has decided he should break the door down."

"Did you try knocking?" asked the mayor.

Hardesty winced irritably.

"Yes, Frank. Several times."

"Move clear, gents," ordered Adams.

He gave quite a performance, charging the door left shoulder first. The impact drove the door inward and, as he stumbled in, he pointed sternly to the open cellblock entrance and informed the banker and the mayor that, if *he* were in charge here, that door would be kept locked.

They followed him into the jailhouse and along the passage to the cell accommodating the lawmen, who had failed to rid themselves of their gags. Brill sat on a bunk with Raddick beside him and stared aghast at Adams and the leading citizens. Oh, the humiliation of it!

"Last I heard, these two losers were arrestin' a couple strangers," Adams triumphantly recalled. "Look at 'em now, gents — locked in their own jail, manacled with their own irons. Some lawmen, huh?" He started back to the office. "I'll go look for keys."

"Damn it, Brill, what's the meaning

of this?" demanded Hardesty.

"They can hear you but, in case you haven't noticed, they can't talk right now," Ball pointed out.

Adams returned with a keyring, unlocked the cell, marched in and de-gagged the lawmen, then curtly asked for the keys to the handcuffs.

"My pants pocket," sighed Raddick.

Brill, after a couple of swallows, earnestly assured Hardesty and the mayor,

"We aren't to blame for this. We were set upon by friends of the Joad brothers, who we'd just arrested."

"Joad brothers?" frowned Ball.

"I got a wire from Deemsville about 'em," said Brill.

"You made an arrest . . . ?" began Hardesty.

"Had our prisoners right there in my office and disarmed," declared Brill. "And then three other jaspers jumped us."

"How'd they get into the office?" challenged Adams.

"Just opened the door and . . . " began Raddick.

"Shuddup, Kell!" groaned Brill.

"Didn't have savvy enough to even lock the door," Adams jeered. "So the other jaspers just sashayed in and took over!"

"I got to get to the telegraph office, got to wire the county sheriff," mumbled Brill.

"Better late than never, Brill?" scowled Hardesty. "Damn it, man, it's dark now. You and your useless deputy have been stuck here most of the afternoon, while those jailbreakers and their friends have put the Ford far behind them. Thanks to your stupidity, they'll *never* be caught!"

The door of the town marshal's office was being repaired and a new lock fitted, a new, fresh-painted shingle hung to the awning, when Brad Tyne rode into Strome's Ford 4 p.m. of the following day.

6

The Approved Suitor

OBSESSED though he was with his craving to apprehend his father's murderer, Tyne could be practical when needs be. No use fooling himself, he reflected, as he idled his weary roan into the Ford's main street. He was as weary as the roan. The pace he had set was tiring him and, right now, he needed to catch up on sleep. Sleep? There had been too little of it since his departure from his hometown; camped by the trail he had slept fitfully, plagued by dreams of the grim past, two funerals, his gnawing sense of loss, his temporary over-dependence on whiskey.

"You'll overnight in a comfortable stall, boy," he muttered to the horse. "And it's a hotel room for me, after

I've done a little checking."

The roan was left at the Adams Livery & Barn, where Pat Kellerby, Adams's cheerful hired hand, assured Tyne he would receive the best of care. From there, Tyne toted his gear to the nearest hotel, the Perrier House, and checked into a ground floor single. Returning to the lobby, he was informed by the desk clerk supper would be available in the dining room from 6.15 onward. Tyne thanked him, propped an elbow on the desk and enquired,

"Any excitement here the last few days?"

"Funny you should ask," grinned the clerk. "Just yesterday a whole lot happened. The marshal and his deputy arrested a couple of strangers at Cowley's Bar and hustled 'em down to the town jail." Tyne's elation was short-lived; the clerk was still talking. "Well, those strangers had friends it seems. The way I heard it, Matt Brill and his deputy no sooner marched 'em into the office than three more strangers showed up an got the drop on 'em. So how do you like this? Mayor Ball and Mister Hardesty the banker found Matt and the deputy locked in a cell, but not till after sundown. Those hard cases made a clean getaway."

"Just what I didn't need to hear," scowled Tyne. "Oh, hell. So near and yet so far."

"You interested in those jailbreakers?" frowned the clerk.

"To put it mildly," nodded Tyne. "Go on. Is that all of it?"

"Mister Hardesty and the mayor got mad," said the clerk. "There was a special council meeting and all the councilmen voted to fire Brill and Kell Raddick."

"So now this town has a new marshal," mused Tyne.

"County sheriff wired his approval," said the clerk. "We're part of Clark County, you see. The county seat's Clark City, big town north east of here. Sure, we got a new marshal, Clem Adams. Until last night, he was . . ."

"Owns a livery stable — I left my horse there," said Tyne.

"Everybody's saying Clem'll do fine," remarked the clerk. "I don't know much about the new deputy they appointed. He hasn't been here long. Helping out at Jerry Bridger's forge till Mayor Ball offered him the job. Looks kind of old to me, but you never can tell, can you? He could be younger than he looks, that Forrester."

"You said Forrester?" Tyne showed quick interest. "First name Luke?"

"Never heard his first name," frowned the clerk. "Grey-haired feller about your size. Keeps pretty much to himself."

"Thanks." Tyne made to leave, then turned back to the desk to ask, "How about a few weeks ago, a month maybe? You happen to notice a couple tall strangers, taller than most?"

"You interested in them too?" The clerk was grinning again. "It was Valentine and Emerson, by golly. Brill and Raddick never saw hide nor hair of 'em. They were only here an hour and a half. That's as long as it took for 'em to tangle with a couple trouble-makers at the Lucky Lulu Saloon. They got prodded into a fight with Rowdy Ray Pearson and Big Boze Jelkie, beat hell out of 'em and quit town again before Brill even heard they'd come by." He shook his head thoughtfully. "That's the damnedest thing. Nobody else asked about those trouble-shooters till just yesterday."

Eyeing him expectantly, Tyne asked, "Can you remember the man who asked you?"

"Just another stranger," shrugged the clerk. "Rough-looking jasper."

Tyne walked slowly from the hotel to the local headquarters of law and order. He was still weary, but only physically, his mind buzzing with questions. Why did the name Forrester register so strongly? He hadn't heard it in years, a lot of years. Well, unless he satisfied his curiosity, supper at the Perrier House could wreak havoc with his digestion. And he could do without that.

En route to the marshal's office, he paused by the batwing doors of a saloon, distracted by the sounds of celebration. There was much laughter, broad grins all round, the dozen locals at the bar congratulating the man wearing the broadest grin of all. A drinker raised his glass and announced gleefully,

"A toast, fellers! To our old buddy Clem Adams, the Ford's new marshal!"

Noting Adams's complacent grin, Tyne moved on. Adams might make it, he supposed. Given time, he could become a useful enough law officer. But the badge was still new on his vest and, right now, he could be no help to an ex-deputy-turned-manhunter.

He reached the law office, climbed to the porch, moved to the door, knocked and tried the knob. It was as new as the door, the lock also, and the new hinges had been oiled. It opened easily. He moved in and, as he closed it behind him, the man prone on the couch by the office's south wall rolled over, nodded to him and raised himself to a sitting position.

"Evening," he said. "If you're looking for the marshal, you'll find him at the Lucky Lulu — celebrating with his buddies."

"It's you I'd as soon talk with, if you're who I hope you are," said Tyne. "Would your given name be Luke?"

Forrester dropped his gaze to the Colt holstered at the newcomer's right side. Seated, he looked to be flat-bellied and maybe leaner than a deputy marshal ought to be. The hair crowning the leathery, impassive visage was ash-grey. But, as Tyne well knew, appearances could be deceptive. This man didn't have to be in his advanced fifties. He could be forty-eight, or thereabouts.

"Who's asking?" he challenged.

"My name's Tyne — Bradford Tyne."

"Sounds..." Forrester thumbed his stubbled jowls, "a mite familiar."

"It's coming back to me now," said Tyne. "Are you Luke Forrester?" The older man nodded slowly. "So, if my name's familiar, you and my father, Jake Tyne, were deputies together a long time ago. Do you also remember Josh Leyland?"

"Remember the name," said Forrester. "Never did meet Leyland. It was at another place your pa and Leyland kept the peace." He studied Tyne wistfully. "So you're Jake's boy? Uh huh. You favor him some."

"Don't get up," said Tyne. He took a chair to the couch, seated himself, and observed, "Back in harness, are you?"

"After quite a time, boy," said Forrester. "Quite a time." He bowed his head. "Guess old Jake talked of me — so you know what happened."

"I was a whole lot younger when he mentioned you, so I don't remember all of it," said Tyne. "Dad didn't speak ill of you, I assure you."

"He wouldn't," said Forrester. "We'd been friends."

"He said something about — a shock, some loss you suffered," Tyne recalled. "Then he said 'It won't lick Luke. He won't stay down long.' I think those were his exact words."

"I stayed down longer than Jake could guess," muttered Forrester. "Because I was a damn fool, boy."

"You're welcome to call me Brad and I wish you would," said Tyne, wincing. "Sad memories, you know? Dad used to call me 'boy' all the time."

"Sorry," said Forrester. "Call me Luke. And heed my advice, Brad. If you ever lose somebody you cared about, don't let it break you, don't take your sorrow to a saloon. That's what I did after my wife ran out on me, took up with a handsomer man, one of those play-actors working a traveling show. Self-pity can be the death of a man. I hit the booze so hard, it cost me my badge and my pride too. Till I came to this town, I was just a trailbum. Only thing I had going for me was I'd dried out. I don't need whiskey so badly nowadays, can take it or leave it."

"Don't be ashamed on my account," begged Tyne. "I've been there, Luke."

"Well, I heard about what happened to Jake," frowned Forrester. "It saddened me, but I didn't make the mistake of getting drunk again. Are you telling me — *you* . . . ?"

"Yes," nodded Tyne. "My mother died a little while later. Too much grief for me, too much anger. I straightened out, but it cost me my badge."

"Still drinking?" Forrester quietly challenged.

"But *I* decide when, and how much," declared Tyne. "You said it and I'm saying it. I can take it or leave it."

"Jake'd appreciate that," said Forrester. "So — uh — what brings you to Strome's Ford? I'm a deputy again, Brad. Seems the mayor of this burg remembered my name. He propositioned me, said this Adams feller's willing enough and strong enough, but he'll do better with an old hand siding him. You looking for something, a lead maybe? I heard the sidewinder who gunned Jake was never identified."

"The law has no suspect in mind,

not officially, but Josh Leyland kept me informed about *my* suspect," Tyne said grimly. "He was here yesterday, Luke, with six others, and two of 'em were the Joad brothers. His name is Jarvis Ames."

"Heard of that sonofabitch," nodded Forrester. "A mean one." He eyed Tyne warily. "You're tagging the whole outfit, all seven? Playing a lone hand?"

"Somehow, sooner or later, there'll be just Ames and me," muttered Tyne. "It's for sure he helped break the Joad boys out of here, so he's answerable to the law anyway. I don't carry a badge any more, probably never will, but I can still try for a citizen's arrest, right? He won't get it in the back, won't get it at all if he surrenders."

"You'd be satisfied to deliver him to the nearest law officer?" prodded Forrester.

"The Joads butchered a storekeeper at Deemsville," said Tyne. "The last marshal of this town arrested them, Ames helped 'em escape, so now he's an accessory to murder. He mightn't hang for what he did to Dad, but he'll certainly hang for that — or rot in prison for the rest of his life. To me, Luke, the important thing is for him to be punished."

"All right," said Forrester. "Old habits die hard, Brad. Helping out at the forge here, I found myself sizing up strangers in town. Didn't see the whole bunch, but I could describe four of 'em. The two Brill and his deputy took out of Cowley's Bar were the Joads I guess. There was another man passed the forge, good-looking, tall, packed his six-shooter at his left with the butt forward . . ."

"That's Ames," scowled Tyne.

"Then you aren't a million miles behind him," said Forrester.

"I'd be moving on rightaway, if I thought I could stay awake in my saddle," sighed Tyne.

"Jake taught you plenty," Forrester opined. "You'd never be fool enough to ride bone-weary and brain-tired, not when you're bird-dogging a killer."

"I'll make an early start tomorrow," said Tyne, rising, offering his hand. "It was good talking to you. And congratulations Luke."

"Too early for . . . " began Forrester, as they shook hands.

"Not too early," Tyne said softly. "On you, that badge looks good."

He retired an hour after finishing his supper and was first to turn out for breakfast next morning. The strawberry roan was as rested as his master. They were on the way by 7.45.

Late afternoon of the following day, while the Texans played cribbage in the J Bar line shack and waited for their supper to cook, Damien Blackwood paid a visit to the Courier office. He was as usual accorded a warm welcome by the editor.

"Good to see you, Damien my boy." Walt Kinstry was always glad to see the handsome cashier from the Merchants and Settlers Bank. And why not? This well-mannered, well-groomed bachelor was seen as his best chance of being rid of pesky Inez. "By golly, you'd have to be the most presentable young feller in all of Kimber County. If that niece of mine knows what's good for her, she'll grab you while you're willing."

"Keep it up, Mister Kinstry," grinned the gentleman caller. "I thrive on encouragement. Now, if Inez would be half as encouraging as her uncle ... "

"It's that damn fool ambition of hers," grouched Kinstry. "Her with her crazy notion of becoming the Charlotte Bronte of America."

"Not giving up on her, are you?" his brother called from the type table.

"Hallo there, Eric," nodded Damien. "No, I don't give up that easily."

"Give it time, Damien," urged Kinstry. He gestured earnestly, so much so that his sweeping arm struck his crutch and sent it clattering to the floor. "Confound Myron Beeby! If he doesn't damn soon rid me of these splints, I'll remove 'em myself!"

"Behave yourself, Walt," chided Clara, entering from the kitchen. "Ah, Damien!"

"Mrs Kinstry, my respects, ma'am." He doffed his derby and treated her to a courtly bow. "With your permission, I will dally a moment with your charming niece — and may I remark you could pass for her sister? I swear, Mrs Kinstry, you don't look old enough to be anybody's aunt."

Eric chuckled. His brother winced and pleaded,

"Don't flatter Clara for pity's sake. She'll get to relishing it and, next thing I know, she'll expect the same from me."

"When it comes to gallantry, Damien could teach you a thing or two," smiled Clara. "Dally as long as you wish, Damien dear. You'll find her writing in the parlor. I don't know if she's attempting another novel. She's very secretive about it."

"Well, I don't like to interrupt her, but . . ." began Damien.

"Interrupt," invited Kinstry. "Keep

on interrupting till she names the day."

"This won't take long," Damien promised, moving to the stairs.

"It doesn't matter how long," Kinstry called after him. "Go to it, boy."

The community's most eligible bachelor climbed the stairs, moved along to the open parlor doorway, entered and aimed a cheery grin at scribbling Inez.

"Good evening, sweetheart," he greeted her. "Will you marry me?"

"Oh, Damien, hallo." Reluctantly, she discarded her pen. "Same answer, Damien. When the right time comes, I'll say yes. I should scold you. I'm in the middle of a most important passage. Writing means *so much* to me, Damien, and . . . "

"The brain is a delicate mechanism," he cautioned, helping himself to a chair. "Don't overwork yours, my dear. Take a break, rest a moment. Well, at least long enough for a little socializing."

"Well," she sighed. "If you insist."

"Word travels fast in this county." He spoke with mock gravity. "I've been told of your visits to a certain isolated spot, namely the line shack at Clear Creek, and now I'm seething with jealousy." He eyed her expectantly. "Doesn't that please you? It's supposed to."

"Jealous?" she challenged. "You don't look jealous, sitting there teasing me. Damien Blackwood, I don't believe you're capable of jealousy."

"Curiosity then," he shrugged.

"Exactly what ... " she asked carefully, "have you heard?"

"Well," he grinned again, "it seems I have rivals for your affections. Rumors are rife, Inez. Those Box Q cowboys who ran foul of your Texas friends couldn't keep their mouths shut. I've no doubt there's a simple explanation for your being seen there — wearing a man's shirt ... "

"There is," she earnestly assured him.

"I don't need to hear it," he said. "You should know I'd never insult you by demanding an explanation."

"No," she nodded. "I must give you

credit, Damien. You're a very patient and understanding person."

"On the other hand, I can't help envying those Texans in whom you're so interested," he said. "Now, if you could become as interested in me . . ."

"There're just friends of mine," she offered. "Much older than you. And, though rough in their ways, they're true gentlemen. Very tactful of you not to demand an explanation, Damien. However, you are entitled to be curious, as I think I should tell you exactly what happened." She recounted the details of her two visits to the line shack, described both mishaps, then frowned indignantly. "Why are you laughing? Stop it!"

"Can't help it!" His laughter subsided to a chuckle. "You know how concerned I am for your welfare. I'm properly grateful you suffered no injury but — twice in the same place — two dunkings?" He gestured apologetically. "Sorry, dear. Don't mean to be unsympathetic but — forgive me for seeing the funny side of it. My beloved Inez, so genteel, so decorous, bouncing into the creek like that — having to dry out in a line shack . . . "

"You're laughing again," she accused.

"Bear with me," he begged. "Would you prefer I had no sense of humor?"

"I guess not," she said with a grudging smile.

"And, about your writing, you know how I feel about it," he reminded her. "I'd never discourage you. If, after you became Mrs Damien Blackwood, you wanted to pursue your writing career, I'd never stand in your way."

"Yes, I'll keep that in mind," she said.

"Now, about your Texas friends, let me remind you I have a relative at Box Q," he said.

"Oh, yes," she nodded. "Mister Starrett the foreman, an uncle on your mother's side."

"So, next time you want to visit Marcie Quiddon, make it a Saturday morning," he suggested. "I'll drive you to Box Q in my father's buggy and, after a short visit, we'll head back to town by way of Clear Creek. I'd be delighted to meet those Texans, Inez. That fight at the Queen of Diamonds is still being discussed — and I missed it. Two against six, and your friends were the winners!"

"They have other qualities, finer qualities," she said reproachfully. "They aren't just common brawlers, Damien."

"Any friends of yours are friends of mine," he assured her. "So what do you say?"

"A buggy ride would be a nice change," she agreed. "Very well, Damien, since you're so eager to meet them, I'll be glad to introduce you. I'll let you know when."

She glanced longingly at her manuscript. He took the hint and rose to leave.

"Really absorbed in this one, are you?" he asked. "Another novel, I presume?"

"Something different," she said. "I'd

prefer not to speak of it until it's finished."

"Whatever you say, Inez," he smiled.

Leaving her, he descended to the office to say his goodbyes to the Kinstrys. His mood was cheerful when, on his way to Elliott Road and the home of his parents, he met a local lawman emerging from the Western Union office. Billy Wright, the younger of Sheriff Hallam's deputies, was of an age with Damien and an old friend, a lean, sandy-haired man of genial disposition. Right now, Wright was preoccupied, so much so that they almost collided. Looking up, recognizing the cashier, he nodded affably.

"'Afternoon, Damien. How's everything?"

"No clouds on my horizon," shrugged Damien. Noting the envelope being shoved into the deputy's jacket pocket, he asked, "Not bad news, I hope?"

"Just something for the sheriff, official stuff," said Wright. "How goes it with you and Inez? She coming round?"

"Only a matter of time, Billy," said Damien. "I don't mind the waiting. We have our whole lives ahead of us."

"Just so long as no other jasper's trying to beat your time," said Wright.

"No," grinned Damien. "As far as I know, I'm her only beau. Tell me something, Billy. Were you at the Queen of Diamonds when those Texans fought off a half-dozen Circle Nine boys?"

"I missed that hassle," Wright said regretfully. "Chris was on duty that night." About to move on, he paused to grin secretively. "You now, it's kind of funny," he confided. "The joke's on Chris, George Hallam too, and even Walt Kinstry. Seems I'm the only one guessed who they are, meaning those sluggers holed up at the Clear Creek line shack." He chuckled softly. "Hey, if old George finds out, he's gonna jump like a coyote with a bullet-burned ass."

"I can keep a secret," offered Damien. "Who do you think they are?"

"It didn't take much figuring," said Wright. "Look, I haven't seen 'em yet, but Ritchie York's barkeep saw the whole ruckus, told me how they held off Madigans's hotheads and beat the tar out of 'em. They're Texan, right? They're uncommon tall and strong — strong enough to win out against a half-dozen plug-uglies? Well, by damn, the only jaspers I ever heard of that could whip triple their weight in a fight are Valentine and Emerson, the trouble-shooters!"

"Those two?" frowned Damien.

"Don't tell me you never heard of 'em," grinned Wright.

"Hasn't everybody?" Damien flashed an answering grin. "Well, this *will* be interesting. Inez became friendly with them, as you've probably heard, so I'll be meeting them soon. We're taking a buggy ride out to Box Q and stopping by Clear Creek on our way home."

"Keep it to yourself," urged Wright. "If Valentine and his buddy want to rest up a while, I figure they're entitled. Not getting in trouble out there, are they, just tending Jacklin's stock? So what

George doesn't know won't hurt him."

"I wonder if Inez knows," mused Damien. "She refers to them as her friends Mister Lawrence and Mister Woodville."

"What matter?" challenged Wright. "What she doesn't know won't hurt *her*. Listen, I got to hustle down to the office before George leaves. See you later, Damien."

Sheriff George Hallam, that austere, craggy-faced veteran, was about to don hat and coat when his junior deputy entered. Chris Parry, with the prospect of walking the sundown to midnight patrol, was taking a shotgun from the rack.

"This just came in," announced Wright, offering the telegram. "Better read it before you call it a day."

Hallam reseated himself, tore the flap of the envelope and extracted the message form. He read the advice, grimaced and told Parry.

"It's from Strome's Ford. The Joad brothers again."

"We got a wire about 'em just a few days ago," frowned Parry. "That killin' at Deemsville."

"Deemsville's a piece west of us," muttered Hallam. "So is Strome's Ford, where the Joads were arrested."

"So that's that," shrugged Parry.

"Not quite, Chris," said Wright.

"They were broken out of the town jail by three other hard cases and everybody's hunch is they're still headed east," growled Hallam. "Elmo Robson, the Clark County sheriff, might organize a search and head 'em off. Then again they could give him the slip. Plenty ways they could dodge a posse between here and Clark County."

"So they could be heading into our territory," said Wright.

"Well, we can't say we haven't been warned," said Hallam, slipping the telegram into a drawer of his desk. "So you know the score, Chris, you too Billy. We stay sharp now. If five strangers show up, I want to know about 'em rightaway. Don't forget that bulletin in the files. We have pictures of the Joads. Study those faces and, from tonight on, keep your eyes peeled."

"If they show up, it'll be the most excitement we've had since that ruckus at the Queen of Diamonds," remarked Parry.

"Bored are you, Chris?" challenged Hallam.

"Hell, no," Parry hastened to assure him. "I go along with you, George. I like it peaceful."

"If the Joads and their buddies're headed east, they could hit Clark City any time," frowned Wright. "That might be as far as they'll come. I mean, if the Clark County law's been tipped off, it could be them nails these jailbreakers."

"Maybe," nodded Hallam. "Or maybe they'll ride by Clark city and Elmo Robson'll be none the wiser — so it could be us sights 'em first." He donned hat and coat and made for the door. "Remember what I said. Stay on your toes from now on."

Alerted by a signpost at a bend of the trail, Jarvis Ames led his men into thick-timbered terrain to the southeast in search of a hideaway. Within the forest, they found a clearing wide enough to accommodate them, after which Ames issued instructions to his chosen scout. It was the day after the Kimber County sheriff had been advised of the murder at Deemsville and the breakout from the Strome's Ford jail.

"Stay on the trail and you should see the lights of Clark City a little while after sundown," Ames told Furth. "Move in quietly, don't draw attention to yourself and, above all, keep your distance from the county lawmen. It should be easy enough for you to find out if our targets are there."

"Or if they *were* there, and how long ago," nodded Furth.

"If anybody gets curious about you, you're making your way to South Dakota," said Ames. "You came up from Colorado and you've never even heard of Deemsville or Strome's Ford.

An old buddy of yours is ramrod of a ranch in the Belle Fourche region and has offered you a job there."

"Sounds good," said Furth. "Ought to fool any nosy citizen gets curious."

"We'll wait for you here," said Ames.

"For how long?" asked Furth.

"This time tomorrow, Bob," Ames said firmly. "Thats as long as we *dare* wait for you." He eyed the Joad's scathingly. "In daylight, we can't afford to stay long in any one place."

"Could be posses out, Bob," warned Hartigan. "So ride wary, huh?"

Furth nodded, remounted and quit the clearing. After rejoining the trail he pressed on to the northeast and, as Ames had predicted, sighted the lights of the county seat around 7 p.m. He rememberd his instructions as he entered Clark City, which proved to be double the size of Strome's Ford. His horse was left tethered outside a small cafe on a side street.

The cafe-owner was one of the inquisitive kind and waited on him personally. He affected the demeanor of a drifting ranch-hand and gave the answers suggested by Ames. And then, before beginning his meal, he grinned a guileless grin and remarked,

"Strangers must be few and far between hereabouts."

"Not all that scarce," said the cafe-owner. "We're on the stage route you know."

"No," said Furth. "I didn't. Should've guessed, huh? It's a big town."

"Growing all the time," said the cafe-owner, moving away. "Growing all the time."

His luck held when, after supper, he patronized a small bar on another side street; he was still keeping a low profile, giving the busy main stem a wide berth. Alone at a corner table, he nursed a shot of rye and sat with chin in hand, feigning weariness and boredom, drawing no attention from the henna-haired percenter in conversation with a townman at a nearby table. Her voice had a nasal, penetrating quality;

the man was just as audible.

"Oh, sure, it was them." She nodded emphatically. "Passed through town so quiet, nobody else pegged 'em for who they were, not even Elmo Robson, and him supposed to be the sharpest sheriff the county ever had. Not him — his deputies either. But, mind you, they didn't linger, Jimmy. They were in this place just long enough to down a couple beers and buy a couple bottles, then they were gone."

"Larry & Stretch." Her companion was intrigued. "No mistake, Ellie?"

"No mistake," she smiled. "Just like their pictures in the papers. And, speakin' of papers, Amos Knapp would've been plenty interested if he'd found out."

"Oh, sure," chuckled the townman. "Too interested for his own good. I hear tell those tumbleweeds tote a heavy grudge against the newspapers."

"Amos could've got his butt kicked," smiled the redhead. "Oh, that Valentine. What a man! Those shoulders!" She rolled her eyes. "I got close enough to size him up. Didn't get to talk to him though. Him and his buddy only talked to Herbie the barkeep. Askin' about the territory farther east."

"I bet they were looking for a quieter place," offered Jimmy. "Bet they're weary of trouble and strife, Ellie. They must be a whole lot older nowadays — aren't we all? Slowing down, I'd reckon, craving to rest easy."

"Maybe," she shrugged. "But they didn't look weary to me. Looked spry. And tough, you know?"

"Kind of sad when you think about it," reflected Jimmy. "Helluva way to live — fighting outlaws year after year, never knowing if their next fight'll be their last."

'Their next fight *will* be their last,' Furth was assuring himself, as he drained his glass and got to his feet.

He quit that quiet bar and, a short time later, was gone from Clark City, headed southwest for the rendezvous in the tall timber. No moon tonight. He had to slow his pace after swinging off the regular trail; the terrain separating him from the forest could not be traveled at speed in darkness.

It was after midnight when he was challenged by a lookout, one of the Joads.

"Me, Furth," he called curtly. "Don't get trigger-happy." As he drew abreast of the elder brother, he asked," Anybody else awake?"

"I wouldn't know," growled Roy Joad, pulling his poncho tighter about him. "I've been patrolin' two hours already, gettin' my ass froze."

Furth rode on into the clearing. Ames, Hartigan and Beavis were rising from their blankets by the time he was dismounting.

"Let's hear it," Ames ordered.

"They passed through," Furth assured him. "Couldn't have stayed longer a couple hours. Wasn't long ago. I think we're gettin' close."

"I have the same feeling," declared Ames, his eyes gleaming. "We needn't wait here any longer. We could be moving east again by . . ."

"Kinda dark," protested Beavis. "We oughta wait till sun-up."

"Just before sun-up'd be safer, and we'd better not travel that trail till we're far ahead of Clark City," opined Hartigan. "What d'you say, Jarv?"

"A few more hours of sleep, then we'll be on our way," decided Ames.

Noon of the following Friday, when the hunters camped by an isolated section of Lamont Creek south of Kimber City, Damien Blackwood, headed home for lunch with his parents, met Inez Durley on Main Street. She was ready to take him up on his offer of a Saturday morning buggy ride to Box Q.

"I'll have an early breakfast, so if you come by for me right afterward . . ."

"As early as you wish," he offered. "The sooner we're through visiting Marcie and Uncle Andy, the sooner

I'll get to meet your heroes at Clear Creek."

By 1.15 p.m., Bob Furth had half-circled the county seat and was making a slow approach to its west side.

7

Prelude to Murder

AT about the same time Ames's spy was entering Kimber City, the duo marked for murder were slumped low in their rocking chairs on the stoop of the line shack. They had disposed of a more than adequate lunch and were supremely content.

"Everything we hoped for, right?" drawled the taller Texan.

"Better," Larry said with relish. "A whole lot better."

He smoked and lazily surveyed the sleek J Bar beeves, the rippling creek and the gentle rises of the Kimber Hills. All tension had left him; he was easier company for Stretch nowadays.

"Just dumb accidents." Stretch happily patted his belly and burped. "The Quiddon gal and her fire-up menfolk.

And Inez gettin' dumped in the creek and us tanglin' with them smart-mouths from Box Q. That kind of stuff never happened here before. Ain't gonna happen again neither. No trouble since, right?"

"No trouble," sighed Larry. "Nothin' to do but tend Milt's special bunch, hunt a little, fish a little and sleep a lot."

"The only way to live," enthused Stretch.

"Ain't that the truth," agreed Larry.

"Who needs excitement anyway?" shrugged Stretch.

"Not us," said Larry.

"Not us," nodded Stretch. "Not nohow." An entire five minutes of companionable silence followed. Then, "You want to do anything 'tween now and suppertime?"

Larry gave that some thought.

"Let's see now. Firewood we don't need, already collected plenty. I don't see none of Milt's special critters strayin' to the brush or the timber. Horses got everything they need. No, I can't think of nothin' I want to do. Might lick you again at cribbage or, if I can work up the energy, might clean and oil my Colt. You?"

"Hind of beef in the root cellar, just a'danglin' down there," mused Stretch. "Might climb on down presently and cut us some steaks for super. Sounds good?"

"Make it four," urged Larry. "Then we got two apiece. I'll peel the potatoes. You want beans or tomatoes?"

"Both," decided Stretch.

"That'll take care of supper," yawned Larry. "Fixin' the steaks'll be your chore. I always liked the way you cook steaks."

Stretch eyed him sidelong.

"You do?"

"Sure," said Larry. "You do a steak just fine."

"You never told me that before," frowned Stretch.

Larry dribbled smoked through his nose.

"I didn't?"

"You never did," declared Stretch. "Ain't that the damnedest thing? All the years we've been driftin' around and shootin' our way out of trouble, we've never talked of such things."

"I guess it didn't seem important," Larry sadly remarked. "Too much strife, stringbean. One ruckus after another. It's been all of twenty years … "

"Think of that," Stretch said in wonderment. "Seems more like twenty months. Maybe because, with us, everything seems to happen fast. We've talked a lot, but mostly about whatever fix we're tryin' to get out of, or how we're gonnna settle some other hombre's trouble. Never get around to talkin' of little things. Like, for instance, d'you got some special reason why you shave the left side of your face first?"

"Is that what I do?" frowned Larry.

"I never yet saw you shave the right side first," said Stretch.

"I didn't notice," shrugged Larry. "But, now that we got nothin' better to do than talk of things that don't matter a damn, there's somethin' about you I'm curious about. When'd you find out you shoot a Colt as good with your left hand as your right?"

"Damned if I remember," said Stretch. "Anything else you're curious about?"

"Uh huh," nodded Larry. "How come you'd as soon own a pinto than any other color horse?"

"Dunno," said Stretch.

"Every so often, you say 'Holy Hannah!' Who's Hannah?" asked Larry. Stretch shrugged and shook his head. "Well, did you pick it up from some other hombre kept sayin' it?"

"Not that I can recollect," said Stretch. "But, listen, we're ol' buddies from way back. So anything you want to know about me, just keep askin'. That's how friends get to savvy each other, runt. Askin' questions."

"Well . . ." Larry rested his bootheels on the porch-rail and closed his eyes. "If I think of anything . . ."

At 2.30 that afternoon, Furth was nursing a drink at the bar of the Queen of Diamonds and engaging a barkeep in casual conversation.

"Neatest lookin' barroom I've seen in a month of Sundays," he remarked. "A lot of this place looks brand-new."

"Carpenters finally finished all the repair work," grinned the barkeep. "Boy, you should've seen it right after the big ruckus. Didn't look so neat then, I'm tellin' you. A shambles it was. We had furniture wrecked, windows busted." He jerked a thumb. "See these shelves back of me? Well, by damn, a Circle Nine waddy got throwed clear over the bar by one of them Texans, hit the wall and brought it all down, shelves, bottles, glasses, everything."

"There's some Texans play rough," Furth said offhandedly.

"Nobody plays rougher'n Valentine and Emerson," declared the barkeep. "That's who they were. Wasn't nobody else pegged 'em. Well, Milt Jacklin maybe. He seemed special interested.

Me now, I pegged 'em right off, saw their pictures in many a newspaper. But Chris Parry, the deputy that hustled in to break it up, *he* didn't recognize 'em. You won't believe this, boy, but there were six of them Circle Nine jaspers crowdin' Valentine and his buddy — and it was *them* took a beatin'. They were good and licked by the time Chris Parry got here."

"I do believe it." Furth forced a grin. "Because I know Larry and Stretch. Haven't seen 'em for years, but I never forget 'em. Good friends of mine. Hey, I'd sure like to see 'em again, if they're still around."

"They'll be around till round-up time," offered the barkeep. "Pike Gillerman, Milt Jacklin's cook, told me Milt hired 'em to guard a little herd up by Clear Creek. J Bar's got a line shack there, you see, and your friends needed some place they could be by 'emselves."

"Nobody else there, just Larry and Stretch?" prodded Furth.

"Lonesomest place in Kimber County," said the barkeep.

"I'd sure appreciate meetin' up with 'em again," muttered Furth, fishing in his pockets. He dropped a banknote on the bar. "Got any sourmash? Make it a quart bottle. By golly, I'm gonna stop by and we'll socialize about old times and it'll be just great. Clear Creek, huh? How do I find the place?"

"Easiest way is stop by the Association office, you know, the Cattlemens Association?" urged the barkeep, as he wrapped the bottle. "Just inside the doorway, left of it, there's a map of the county shows every spread, the range markers and where the line shacks are."

Furth thanked him amiably, drained his glass and left to find the Association office. En route, he stopped by the lobby of a hotel and, while the desk-clerk was distracted by a complaining guest, helped himself to a sheet of the hotel's stationery. He spent almost a quarter-hour in careful study of the map at the Association office, marking the location of the Clear Creek shack and, with a stub of pencil, charting a route by which seven strange riders could circle the county seat and advance on Clear Creek from the west without trespassing on neighboring range.

Headed for where his horse waited, he paused halfway along a side alley to give thought to the task ahead. Others had underestimated the battle-wise trouble-shooters and suffered for their presumption and over-confidence. Think one jump ahead, he cautioned himself. No matter how stealthy their approach, their intended victims could be forewarned. The nicker of a nervous horse, the sudden restlessness of the cattle under guard could do it, could alert the Texans, who would probably retreat into the shack and fort up to hold off an attack. What did he know of line shacks?

"Far south, they'd be nothin' better than adobes," he reflected. "This far north, timber, nothin' surer. Log cabin, maybe, or clapboard."

From the alley, he made his way to the nearest general store; it was only a short distance but, until he reached the entrance, he kept his eyes peeled for local lawmen. His purchase aroused no curiosity. Coal-oil was a staple of the times; without it lamps were useless.

It was 4 p.m. when he rejoined the six men waiting him at the rendezvous.

"Fast work," Brandon remarked with an approving grin. "What's the good word? We travelin' on again?"

"No." Furth traded stares with Ames. "We finish it here in Kimber County."

"Found the bastards!" breathed Hartigan.

"In town?" demanded Ames.

"Far out of town, far north," declared Furth. "A lonesome place. They got it all to themselves and nobody ever goes there. I'm talkin' about a line shack by a creek, Jarv."

"In an isolated area?" Ames swore softly. "It sounds perfect!"

"Thinkin' of burnin' 'em out?" grinned

Beavis, noting the can secured to Furth's saddle.

"Might come to that," insisted Furth.

"That's what I call initiative," said Ames, frowning at the Joads. "Bob's thinking ahead. They could defend that shack if they sighted or heard us. Vigilance is second nature to Valentine and Emerson. While their ammunition lasts, they could hold us off for a long time."

"It'd help if we knew the layout," suggested Hartigan.

"Here's the layout." Furth dismounted and handed the folded paper to Ames. "I found a map and copied all we need to know. We stick to that route, we'll stay far clear of town and make it to thick timber west of the shack."

While Ames studied Furth's handiwork, Hartigan made him an offer.

"I'm volunteerin', Jarv. Suppose now we don't reach the timber till after sundown? I figure I could pussyfoot all the way to the shack and douse the walls. Then all we'd need is firebrands.

Whenever we're ready, we could throw our brands right where they'll do the most good for us." He bared his teeth. "Gives 'em two choices. Stay in there and burn with the shack, or run out for us to gun 'em down."

"Quite an idea, Lafe," muttered Ames. "Very appealing."

"Thought you'd like it," grinned Hartigan.

"Keep this." Ames returned the map to Furth. "Here's the plan. We eat now, get moving again after sundown. No guessing when we'll reach the timber west of the shack. When we do, I'll size up the situation and decide our strategy. From here to the timber, Bob will be our guide."

"Finally ram 'em to ground," mumbled Beavis, his voice shaking with emotion. "By tomorrow I'll be squarin' accounts for Jed!"

"We all have a score to settle," nodded Ames. "I want them to know why they have to die. That's important to me, and you must feel the same way. They have to know we've sentenced them to death and why."

"Yeah," nodded Brandon. "That's important, real important. I used to have two brothers, and I aim to remind Valentine of 'em."

With Clark City many miles behind him, Brad Tyne nightcamped by a waterhole west of the Kimber County line, looked to the feeding and watering of his horse and, after preparing an austere supper, pondered his situation. Information gleaned in Clark City left him in no doubt his quarry were still eastbound. Having been alerted by telegraph of the Strome's Ford jailbreak, Sheriff Robson and his deputies were checking on all strangers; he had himself been questioned.

'Which doesn't mean they could check on every stranger sneaking into town,' he reflected while eating. 'Ames is no fool. After what happened at Strome's Ford, he wouldn't lead his gang into Clark City or any other town. He'd send a spy in, if he's on a man-hunt, and I think he is. Why would they ask about those Texans? Valentine and Emerson have no outlaw friends — just enemies. It'll probably be the same when I reach the next town on this trail, but I have to be sure.'

For how long could he force himself to remain inactive? He answered that question at midnight by rolling from his blankets and kicking dirt onto his fire. The roan was well rested and the roan's owner had slept long enough. He saddled up, secured his gear and pressed on toward the seat of Kimber County.

At sundown, while Larry lounged in the open shack doorway, staring out at Milt Jacklin's prized stock, Stretch climbed out of the cellar and cheerily challenged,

"Good enough?"

Larry glanced over his shoulder. His partner had nudged the trapdoor back into position and was proudly exhibiting four sizeable steaks.

"Couldn't be better, amigo," he said

approvingly. "Beans and tomatoes in the pot. I got the skillet sizzlin' and it's ready as it'll ever be, so do your doggonedest."

The taller Texan made a small ceremony of depositing the steaks in the big pan. The sizzling sound was suddenly louder, and music to their ears. Blissfully content, the veterans sniffed appetizing aromas and traded grins.

"Now I ask you," said Stretch. "What price driftin' aimless in Wyomin' this time of year? Ain't this better?"

"Beats roastin' jackrabbit over a campfire," remarked Larry.

"I tell you, runt, I could stay here forever," enthused Stretch. "We got it made. Snug shelter, easy chores, plenty grub, nobody botherin' us ... "

"We'll be sorry to go." Larry closed the door and seated himself at the table. "But go we will, and you know it. After round-up, Milt'll pay us off. He'll likely invite us to stay on, and maybe we'll be tempted. We won't enjoy quittin' this territory, but we'll do it anyway."

"You had to remind me," chided Stretch.

"Ain't tellin' you what you don't already know," shrugged Larry.

"Yeah, sure." Stretch used a long fork to turn the steaks, then dropped grinds in the coffeepot, filled it with water and set it on the stove. "But, you know, it's got to happen sometime."

"What's got to happen?" asked Larry.

"We can't ramble forever," muttered Stretch. "Some mornin', we're gonna wake up beside of a campfire that's gone cold, or maybe in a room in some cowtown hotel, and we're gonna look at ourselves and find we've grown old. I mean *too* old, Larry. And slowed down. Maybe a mite rheumaticky and maybe with old wounds givin' us hell, near cripplin' us."

"Real cheerful notions you get," complained Larry.

"Got to happen," warned Stretch.

"Uh huh," grunted Larry. "Some time."

"So then what?" frowned Stretch.

"We'll be over the hill — no use foolin' ourselves. Some smart-ass gunslick half our age — or even younger — decides it's time *he* got to be famous, and . . . "

"There'd be more'n one of 'em," scowled Larry.

"And we won't be as fast as we used to be," fretted Stretch. "Is that how you want to check out? Gunned down by a proddy young'un with a hair-trigger six-gun?"

"We start broodin' about how we're gonna get it, we'll be miserable company for each other," grouched Larry. "It'll happen when it happens, beanpole. When your number's up, that's it."

"Don't have to be like that for us," argued Stretch. "Why don't we agree on it? If it gets to where our eyes ain't so keen and our gun-arms failin' us — if we just *know* we're past our prime — we head on back to the old Lone Star. Wouldn't you as soon die in Texas — in bed — and get buried in Texas ground? Me now, I don't crave to get planted in some foreign place."

"Yeah, okay, it's a deal," Larry said irritably. "How're them steaks comin' along?"

"How d'you like yours?" asked Stretch.

"You know how I like mine," said Larry. "On the plate."

The wind was blowing from the east when, sometime later, the man-hunters dismounted at the west side of the timber, removed their spurs and began leading their animals through the trees. At the east edge of the forest, Brandon took charge of the horses, tying them, then emptying saddle-scabbards and distributing rifles. There was bright moonlight, much to Ames's satisfaction. Eagerly, he surveyed the terrain east, studying the shack, the lamplight glowing from a south window, the rampart of boulders further south, the bedded herd east and, to the north, the creek and the hills beyond.

"Open ground all around the shack," he observed.

"'Cept for that line of rocks," said

Hartigan, hunkering beside him. "Good cover, them rocks."

"Shack's mostly clapboard," Furth noted. "It'll burn, Jarv. It'll burn good."

"Well — uh — how're we gonna do it?" demanded Roy Joad, as impatient as ever.

"How long we gonna wait?" frowned his brother.

"I've decided we'll attack in daylight," muttered Ames. "We have clear moonlight right now, but I don't trust it. All it takes is a cloudbank. Pitch dark could help our targets — and I don't plan on giving them any kind of chance. We've come too far to be cheated. This time, they have to die."

"Wait for 'em to bunk down," guessed Hartigan.

"Sounds good," grinned Beavis.

"Some time after they kill their lamp," said Ames. "When we can be sure they're sleeping, Lafe will sneak over there and douse the walls. But first we'll rig the firebrands." He glanced to the rocks again. "And we'll attack from there. Just the right distance from the shack and the ideal stakeout. They can't come out unbeknowns to us."

"Some turkey-shoot this'll be," chuckled Brandon. "Worth all the travelin', huh? All the waitin'?"

"Firebrands," said Ames.

They had collected dry sapling rods of suitable length on their way to the timber. To the ends of those rods, they now tied bandanas or cloth torn from shirttails. Just before Hartigan started for the shack, the brands would be dipped into the inflammable liquid.

Forty-five minutes later, the lamp was extinguished, the Texans climbing into bunks. Ames waited another hour before giving the order to move. The brands were saturated, after which Hartigan discarded the can's cap and broke from the timber to creep to the shack. He proceeded slowly and cautiously while Ames and the others, toting rifles and firebrands, made just as slowly for the rocks.

The shack's occupants were in deep

sleep when Hartigan doused its south and rear walls. By then, his cohorts were concealed behind the rampart of boulders. He started in that direction, disciplining himself against breaking into a run. No need, he assured himself.

A few more minutes and he was clambering over the rocks to squat beside Ames and retrieve his rifle from Brandon.

"Shingled roof," he cheerfully informed Ames. "When we get to throwin' them brands, we oughta aim one for the roof."

"No more talk," Ames said softly. "The rest of you might as well rest. I'll stay awake — couldn't sleep anyway."

"Come sun-up, them heroes rouse," muttered Furth. "For the last time."

Dawn had not broken when Tyne idled his tired mount into Kimber City's main street. He made first for a livery, where he left the animal in care of a stablehand just coming awake.

"Take care of my gear." He tipped the stablehand and asked, "Which diner opens earliest in this town? I'm hungry."

"Leroy Castle's place," offered the stablehand. "A block uptown, other side of the street. It's called the Bluejay."

When Tyne found it, the Bluejay's front door was opening and an early riser, Deputy Billy Wright, trading greetings with the as yet unshaven proprietor.

"You and your appetite that can't wait," grouched Castle, as Wright followed him in.

"Bacon, three eggs, stack of hot biscuits . . ." recited Wright.

"I know your order by heart," mumbled Castle. En route to his kitchen, he paused to eye the stranger now entering. "Hell's sakes, don't anybody sleep late any more?"

"I'll take the same," Tyne told him. Wright was seated and studying him warily. He nodded politely. "I'll share your table if you don't mind. You'll want to talk to me anyway, right?"

"Well," frowned Wright. "We're some

curious about strangers passing through."

"You and every badge along my route," said Tyne. He hung his hat and seated himself opposite the deputy. "Because the Joads are still headed east."

"We'd better start with your name," suggested Wright.

"You're welcome to it," said Tyne. "But we'll start with my profession — and what used to be my profession. I was deputy town marshal of Beauvais, Utah, for some years. Now I deal faro in a Beauvais saloon. I'm Brad Tyne. You won't have heard of me, but my father was quite well known."

"I've heard Sheriff Hallam mention a lawman of that name," said Wright.

"Jake Tyne, my father," said Tyne.

"Well," said Wright. "I guess we don't have to worry about you."

"If you need to check on me, you could wire my name and description to Sheriff Leyland of Twin Forks, Nevada," offered Tyne.

He said nothing more until their

breakfast arrived. After an egg and a rasher of bacon, he decided on a short-cut question. The Ames gang's interest in the Texas Trouble-shooters intrigued him; he was ready to play a hunch.

"I won't ask if you've heard of Valentine and Emerson — dumb question to put to any lawman," he said casually. "But it seems they passed through a few towns west of this territory. You seen anything of them?" He munched on another mouthful and frowned at the deputy. "Did I say something funny?"

"Kind of a private joke," chuckled Wright. "There was a ruckus here, big one at a saloon uptown, half-dozen local cowhands trying to beat up you-know-who and getting the worst of it. The funny part is, when my partner got there, the fight was over and those sonofagun Texans were still on their feet — Chris didn't recognize them. My boss, Sheriff Hallam, *he* doesn't know who's manning Milt Jacklin's line shack at Clear Creek. Seems I'm the only one realized it had to be Valentine and Emerson. You heard of any other two fiddlefoots who could win out against that much opposition?"

"Typical of Valentine and Emerson," agreed Tyne. "Manning a line shack you said? How do I find the place?"

"You don't carry a badge any more," countered Wright. "So what would you want with them?"

"I'm still curious, never did meet them," said Tyne. "And, since I'm in the neighborhood, why not?"

"I think before I told you how to find your way to Clear Creek, I'd have to know exactly how you feel about Valentine and his partner," decided Wright. "Personally now, there's no chip on my shoulder — and I've worn this badge quite a time, friend. I got no quarrel with any drifter who's nailed more law-breakers than any newspaperman could tally. But how about *you*?"

"My father never encountered them

either," Tyne told him. "I go along with his opinion of them — and he admired them."

"No old grudges?" prodded Wright. "They never beat you to an owlhoot you were set on capturing?"

"No," said Tyne. "And, if they ever had, I'd have thanked them for saving me the trouble. You can believe that."

Their plates were clean. Castle delivered their coffee. Wright, under the influence of Tyne's unwavering gaze, decided he was all he claimed to be. He swigged coffee and offered directions.

"Easiest way for you would be to head north to Clear Creek, then follow it east. When you sight the Kimber Hills, the shack will be to your right. It's easy to spot. You'll see Milt Jacklin's special herd on the flats further east and, this time of year, you can bet those Texans'll be showing smoke. Unless they keep the stove going, the shack would be cold as a cardsharp's heart."

"Thanks," said Tyne. "It's a chance to satisfy my curiosity. Might never happen again, so I'll ride out there and look 'em over."

"One thing you don't have to be curious about," remarked Wright. "That question a lot of people ask — are they as tough as they used to be? I talked to a friend who was in the Queen of Diamonds when the fight started. He saw it all, Tyne. And nobody'll convince *him* they're slowing down."

"But nobody lasts forever," Tyne said soberly. "Time won't stand still, you know. It just now occurred to me I was only knee-high when I first heard my father speak of the Lone Star Hellions."

"Yeah," nodded Wright. "I was many a year younger when I first heard of them."

Tyne was first to finish. Rising, he dropped money on the table and nodded affably.

"On me."

Returning to the livery stable, he paid for the rental of a dun colt, saddled it and secured his sheathed rifle. Then his journey to Clear Creek began while, behind the rocks south of the line shack, the seven avengers looked to their weapons and prepared to ignite and hurl firebrands.

"I'll announce us first," Ames insisted. "We're agreed, aren't we? They have to know why they're going to die?"

"That'll be the best part," grinned Brandon.

"Go ahead, Jarv," urged Hartigan. "I wouldn't have it any other way."

The Texans were out of their bunks and tugging their boots on when they heard the shouted challenge. They were perplexed, but wary too. Automatically, they reached for and strapped on their sidearms.

"Valentine — and Emerson — we know you're in there!" Ames called triumphantly. "It's retribution time! We're here for a final reckoning!"

"What in tarnation . . . ?" began Stretch.

"Let's find out," frowned Larry,

moving to the door.

"Watch yourself," cautioned Stretch. He took up his Winchester while Larry turned the knob. The door was opened just a few inches.

"The rocks," he said softly. "He's hollerin' from back of that line of rocks."

"He ain't alone," opined Stretch.

"Question is — how many of 'em?" muttered Larry. He stood clear of the door and answered Ames. "What's this all about?"

"I told you!" bellowed Ames. "Retribution! I'll name some men you've probably forgotten, Valentine. Al Drood!"

"Jed Beavis!" yelled Beavis. "My brother!"

"And my brother Gilly!" raged Furth.

"Red Calnan!" snarled Hartigan. "Cousin of mine!"

"I had two brothers!" roared Brandon.

"And we're kin of Finn Garson!" cried Roy Joad.

Larry frowned at Stretch, who

grimaced in disgust.

"Murder raid, runt. Quite a bunch of 'em out there — all hankerin' to settle old debts."

"Remember how peaceable it used to be here?" Larry asked bitterly.

"Not any more I don't," growled Stretch.

"Your time has come!" Ames jubilantly announced.

"Don't bet on it!" Larry retorted.

Rifles barked from the rocks. He cursed, pushed the door shut and, as bullets slammed into it, dropped to all fours and crawled across to where he had left his rifle. The side window was shattered by a hail of lead and, undaunted, Stretch positioned himself there with his Winchester barking. His fast-triggered burst scored no hits, but the slugs ricocheted off the boulders, forcing the attackers to duck in haste.

The battle of Clear Creek had begun and the J Bar beeves were uneasy now, bawling a protest, milling restlessly. Larry found and readied his rifle, crawled back to the door, reached up to turn the knob again, then edged clear as it half-opened. Just as he anticipated he drew fire. Three bullets hurtled through the opening to plow into the sides of bunks and, scowling defiantly, he moved to the threshold and got his rifle working, his first four shots convincing the raiders there would be no surrender. Surrender? The thought never occured to the case-hardened Texans.

"Now Jarv?" prodded Hartigan

"Now," nodded Ames. "Get 'em burning and, when you're ready to throw, we'll give you cover."

A match flared and was touched to the damp ends of five brands. The brands ignited and, as Hartigan, Furth and Brandon hurled them, Ames, Beavis and the Joads rose up with their rifles clamoring. The first brand landed on the shack's shingled roof. The second and third fell close to the rear wall, the fourth and fifth went to ground close enough to the south wall to ignite it.

Now, spooked by the din of gunfire,

the herd began moving. In a matter of moments, J Bar's best steers were southbound.

Reloading their rifles, the Texans cocked ears to the ugly crackling sounds. Larry raised his eyes and said grimly.

"Plain enough, huh? They mean to burn us out of here."

"They could do it," winced Stretch. "This shack'll burn fast and, if we stay put, we'll burn with it."

"The horses!" gasped Larry. "I got to turn 'em loose!"

"Hell, runt!" Stretch protested. "Step outside that door and you're done for!"

8

To the Death

CROUCHED left of the doorway, Larry discarded his rifle and drew his Colt.

"Those critters're screamin' already," he muttered. "You want to hear 'em die? They'll burn for sure if I don't get 'em out of there. That's all I have to do. Once out of the barn, they'll run."

Stretch levered a shell into his breech and nodded.

"All right, make your move. I'll be in that doorway soon as you're clear of it, cover you the best way I can."

"Best way is get a clear bead on one of 'em," urged Larry.

"As if you need to tell me," growled Stretch, moving toward him. "Okay? Any time you're ready."

Larry emerged and darted toward

the barn with his Colt booming. At once, Stretch was manning the doorway, leveling his Winchester. He fired at the first raised head and was sure he'd hit his mark, but kept firing. Bullets whined past him, too close for comfort, and still he kept his rifle working, while Larry did what he had to do.

Released, the J Bar horses took off at a frantic gallop, and now Larry made his return dash. He reached the doorway to collide with his partner, the impact putting them face-down on the floor, side by side and coughing. Smoke was penetrating fast. All four walls were afire.

"You hit?" panted Larry, rolling over to reload his sixgun.

"Not yet," frowned Stretch. "But you are. Don't you know it? Ain't you hurtin'?"

Larry raised his eyes again and not a moment too soon.

"Move your ass!" he gasped.

They rolled and a blazing shingle dropped between them. Cursing, Larry sat up and began knotting his bandana about the shallow gash in his left forearm. He coughed again, his eyes stinging and watering.

Behind the rocks, Noah Joad was hunkered beside his sprawled brother and cursing obscenely. Ames and the other men reloaded, keeping their eyes on the burning shack.

"He's dead!" wailed Joad. "*Look* at him! They got Roy — in the head! Damn 'em to hell — I *gotta kill 'em*!"

"We're all sorry about Roy, kid," growled Hartigan. "But we knew there'd be risks."

"He didn't die for nothin'," Beavis offered as consolation. "Today's the day *they're* gonna die."

"Your choice, heroes!" bellowed Ames. "Come out and face us — or stay in there and fry!"

Larry crawled closer to the doorway, gulped air and retorted at the full strength of his lungs.

"If I believed you bastards'd have

guts enough to move out from those rocks, I'd come out sure enough!"

"Sure-thing killers!" taunted Stretch.

"It's you who must die!" roared Ames. "We're here to *finish* you! I've sentenced you to death as just punishment — vengeance for our friends and kin — comfort for their graves!"

The wind blew a gust of wind into the shack, temporarily shifting the smoke plaguing the defenders. Stretch gulped gratefully and managed a short remark.

"Sounds loco, don't he? Helluva way for us to go, runt."

"I don't like it either," muttered Larry.

Stretch crawled closer to him, his eyes smarting.

"You know they ain't gonna break from them rocks. We run out, we'd be lucky to down just one of 'em. The others'd cut us down fast."

A compulsive warrior in any and all circumstances, Larry savagely declared,

"I'd as soon down 'em all!"

"Might be our time's come." Stretch said it resignedly. "We can't hold out much longer. Neither can them walls. But we could be dead before the roof comes down on us. Smoke's gettin' thicker — gonna smother us."

"You want to chance it?" frowned Larry.

"Chance what?" asked Stretch.

"We can't stay here and burn — can't run out and get picked off like a couple spooked jackrabbits," declared Larry. "But there's a third choice. We go underground."

"The root cellar?" blinked Stretch.

"Maybe a long chance," warned Larry. "Could be hell-hot down there — no way of guessin' from up here. And for all we know, the cellar could fill with smoke and we'd smother anyway." Two more shingles fell, scattering sparks. Stretch looked around. There was as much flame as smoke now. He could see the trapdoor, but only just.

"No time for flippin' a dime nor for talkin' about it," he mumbled. "If we're gonna chance it — it has to be *now*."

"Move," urged Larry.

They crawled laboriously, he overturning the table, Stretch thrusting a chair aside. Reaching the trapdoor, he raised it. Feet-first he lowered himself through the opening. His booted feet found contact with the rungs of the ladder and he descended with Larry following. Larry, poised on the fifth rung, crouched, felt for the trapdoor and pulled it back into position. Then he finished his descent.

It was pitch-dark down here until Stretch scratched a match and touched it to a tallow candle. They squatted by the ladder, sweating, trading stares.

"Not so hot," observed Stretch. "You breathin' easier? I sure am. No smoke down here."

"We left our rifles up there," grouched Larry.

"That ain't all," sighed Stretch. "Our hats, all our spare duds, everything in our saddlebags and packrolls . . ."

"I just remembered somethin' makes

me feel a mite happier," said Larry.

"Don't keep it a secret," begged Stretch. "Be nice if we *both* felt a mite happier."

Larry patted the butt of his loaded and holstered Colt. Stretch grinned, suddenly comforted by the feel of his own shellbelt girding his loins, the weight of his matched .45s.

"If we get out of here — after the shack's burned down," Larry said softly. "If they've broke cover by the time we see daylight ..."

"Uh huh," grunted Stretch. "They crave to butcher us — but they'll have to do it the hard way."

"Sonsabitches." Bitterly, Larry vented his resentment. "Sure-thing killers."

"Polecats," sneered Stretch.

"Can they call 'emselves men — crowdin' us this way?" scowled Larry. "Stay and burn or come out and get gunned down. That's the choice they gave us — keepin' all that rock 'tween them and us. Safe cover for them. No fightin' chance for us."

"Real heroes," Stretch said scathingly. "Hey, you remember any of them names they hollered at us? Beavis — Calnan . . . ?"

"Been too many we had to kill," said Larry. "Who could remember? Most of 'em, we never *knew* their names." He winced to the thudding, crackling sounds. Above them, the fire raged. The walls were collapsing. Soon enough, the roof would come down. Another thought occurred to him. "While we can breathe down here, there's somethin' else makes me happy."

"I'd admire to be happy too," said Stretch.

"It's many a long hour since we last ate," Larry reminded him. "No cooked grub down here, but plenty canned stuff. And old Pike said there's booze."

"Rum," recalled Stretch. "And a keg of whiskey. So what're we waitin' for?"

While the raiders watched the shack burn, Stretch found a couple of cans of pork and beans and some discarded tools, a spade, a claw-hammer. He managed to open the cans by the time Larry located the keg and pulled the stopper. They hunkered again, satisfying their hunger with pork and beans, eating off their jackknives, taking turns to swig whiskey from the keg.

Tyne, meanwhile, was riding the south bank of the creek with extreme caution, alerted by the distant clatter of gunfire some time before. His Winchester was unsheathed. He held his rein lefthanded, the rifle hefted by its magazine, and cocked.

No more shooting could he hear, but he was not discounting the possible significance of the smoke rising away to his right. Too much of it to be belching from the stack of a line shack or rising from a campfire.

When he reached the section at which southbound riders usually forded, one quick glance assured him he should ride no further, not if he wanted to keep his presence a secret. He reined up, dismounted and tied his rented colt on the north side of a thicket close to the bank. Then, bent double, he crept away from the bank to seek a vantagepoint. His choice was a patch of soft grass shaded by an overhang of brush. He lay prone on it and scanned the scene further south.

No sign of cattle. Not a horse in sight. Flame and smoke rose from what used to be the line shack, barn and privvy. And what of the line of boulders to the left and beyond the fire? He saw heads raised. Men had taken cover there and were staring toward the crumbling shack.

'You're waiting,' he realized. 'And now *I* must wait — hoping one of you is Jarvis Ames.'

The smoke was subsiding; flaming beams had become smoldering embers.

"Beautiful, huh?" leered Brandon.

"I have one regret," muttered Ames. "It would have been music to my ears but, of course, they had to disappoint me."

"What're you talkin' about?" demanded Hartigan.

"They're dead, Jarv," said Furth. "They burned. That's what matters."

"I wanted to hear them scream as they burned!" Ames said harshly. "Damn them — they had to be brave about it, too stubborn to cry in agony, heroes to the end!"

"Won't be much left of 'em" opined Beavis.

"Not much at all," scowled Noah Joad. "But I gotta see it — for Roy's sake."

"You can spit on what's left of 'em, if it'll pleasure you any," grinned Hartigan.

"It'll pleasure me," Joad assured him.

"Better we wait a while, give that mess time to cool," said Furth.

In the cellar, Stretch stoppered the whiskey keg and grimaced uneasily. Through the smoldering floorboards above, smoke was drifting in.

"Time to go, runt," he muttered.

"Well, what the hell?" shrugged Larry. "I crave daylight anyway." He climbed the ladder. Staring upward, he noted the charred condition of the trapdoor. "Pass up that spade." Stretch obliged. He grasped its lower part, pressed the handle against the blackened wood and shoved hard. Nothing budged. Sweat beaded on his brow, but he resisted panic. "Find somethin' to stand on so you can help me push."

"We pinned down?" frowned Stretch.

"Only for as long as it takes to force our way up and out," said Larry.

The taller Texan found a box, then another, positioned them by the bottom of the ladder, mounted them and got a grip on the spade.

"Ready when you are, runt."

"Bueno," grunted Larry. "Now we *push*."

At this moment, Hartigan rose to his full height and announced,

"I'm for takin' a look."

"I'm with you," said Brandon.

"Me too," Joad said eagerly.

"All right," nodded Ames. "We needn't wait any longer."

The six began clambering over the rocks, while the Texans mustered their muscle-power for a last upward thrust. At last the smoldering rafter that had fallen across the trapdoor was dislodged and, thirty yards from the mound of charred rubble, Ames and his cronies jerked to a shocked halt.

They were seeing it, but in stunned disbelief. It was as though the tall men were rising from the dead, looming into clear view, faces blackened, clothes begrimed, ash cascading from their heads and shoulders.

But none of that ash got into their eyes to obscure their vision. The Texans had a clear view of six of the killers who had sentenced them to a fiery death. Their blood was up. But, even now, Stretch was still Stretch, confounding the enemy in his own unique way.

"Peekaboo," he called to them. "You lookin' for us?"

"They're *alive*!" cried Joad.

"Damn you, Valentine!" yelled Beavis. "This is for Jed!"

He wasn't first to fill his hand. Ames and the others were drawing fast, but Larry's and both of his partner's were clear of leather and booming already. It was a fast and bloody shootout, the veteran troubleshooters coldly deliberate and deadly accurate, their would-be killers unnerved, infuriated and out-classed.

Beavis, the first to die, reeled from the impact of a .45 slug hitting him dead centre. As he pitched to the dust, Noah Joad, mortally wounded by the second shot from Stretch's lefthand colt, loosed a wail and lurched drunkenly with his chest bloody. Stretch flinched from the hot breath of a slug fanning his right ear, sighted on the shooter and squeezed both triggers. Both bullets hit their mark, Brandon, who hurtled backward to collapse and sprawl grotesquely.

Hartigan and Furth were shooting fast, Ames watching Larry, waiting his chance to draw a clear bead. Firing while falling, Stretch creased Hartigan, who started convulsively, dropped his pistol and, to the accompaniment of a howl of agony, clasped both hands to the angry slash of red at his left side. Furth fanned his weapon at Larry, who crouched and fired from the hip. Something ugly happened to Furth's head; he was dead before he hit ground. And Stretch was down, conscious, but seeing everything through a haze of pain, bleeding from his left calf.

As Ames lined his weapon on him, Larry cocked, triggered and swore in frustration; his hammer had snapped on a spent shell. He dodged frantically, yelled to Stretch to throw him a gun and heard Ames's startled gasp. Simultaneously, the echo of a rifle-shot reached him, and now his gaze fixed on the sixth gunman's handsome but contorted face.

Ames bowed his head a moment to stare uncomprehendingly at the torn section of his right pants-leg and the blood trickling through. Then he straightened up, glared wildly about and raised his pistol again. With the echo of the second rifle-shot he backstepped jerkily, bowing his head again. His shirtfront showed a red blur. His gunhand was sagging, though he strove to raise it. He fought hard to stay upright, but now his legs buckled. As he fell, he glared balefully at Larry. Then he was down and dead with his face in the dirt.

With trembling hands, Larry ejected his spent shells and tugged replacements from his belt. Hartigan, the only killer still alive, had lost consciousness. Not so Stretch, who complained,

"Leg's — givin' me hell."

"I'm good and alive," Larry assured him, turning to stare northward. "Alive enough to do somethin' about your wound."

"You sound like you don't believe what you're tellin' me," mumbled Stretch.

"Still tryin' to convince myself," frowned Larry. "I ought to be gravebait, amigo. That last bastard had me cold — till some sharpshooter dropped him from up by the creek. Uh huh. Here he comes. Remind me to thank him."

"Where you goin'?" groaned Stretch.

"Goin' back down for that keg," muttered Larry. "We didn't empty it, and we're gonna need what's left in it."

When, a few minutes later, he climbed out of the cellar toting the whiskey, Tyne was dismounting beside Stretch. The ex-deputy did not at first check on the Texans; he moved to one of the bodies, rolled it over and, for a long moment, studied a contorted, dust-caked face.

"I owe you one — whoever you are," Larry called to him.

"Name of Tyne," said the newcomer, turning towards Stretch. "Brad to my friends."

At the J Bar headquarters meanwhile, Milt Jacklin was bellowing for somebody to fetch him a saddled horse. His foreman and a half-dozen hands were already mounted because, from an upstairs window of the ranch-house,

Milt had been a shocked witness to the arrival of his prized stock; all the runaways from the Clear Creek graze had kept coming, not stopping till they reached the work corrals.

"Has to mean trouble at Clear Creek," he growled at Dan Corrie. "Would a couple top hands let my best steers up and quit — if they could help it?"

"Now what, Slim?" Corrie called the challenge to a rider fast approaching. "You and McCardle're supposed to be fence-fixing' in the west quarter."

"Must be somethin' happened up to Clear Creek." The cowhand reined up to report, "Marty and me headed off four saddlers — J Bar they are — and I could swear they're the same critters them new hands chose from our string."

"Damn and blast!" fumed Milt. "*C'mon*, for pity's sakes!"

The J Bar party raised dust in the area fronting the ranchhouse, spurring hastily-saddled horses to a hard run while, at the scene of the shootout, Tyne finished confiding in the Texans, accepted a shot from the keg and contributed a clean bandana for the binding of Stretch's wound. The taller trouble-shooter had suffered no bone damage, a bullet having penetrated a calf, but he would be inactive for some time.

"Feels easier now?" Larry asked solicitously.

"Feels like it's afire," grouched Stretch. "Raw whiskey sure makes a wound smart."

"You got enough of it in your belly to make the hurtin' worthwhile," suggested Larry. He thanked Tyne again for his life, adding, "That wasn't my first close call, but you never do get used to it. If you'd triggered a split second later, I'd be dead as him."

"Just so you'll understand," said Tyne. "I had no way of knowing your gun was empty."

"You'd have cut loose at him anyway," nodded Larry, "on account of it was him gut-shot your pa."

"I call that a damn good reason,"

muttered Stretch. "Well now, runt, look at us. Toilworn and burnt out. Got nothin' left but the dirty duds on our backs and — hey — your wallet in your pants?"

"Uh huh," grunted Larry. He patted his hip pocket reassuringly. "We still got our bankroll, our Colts and our horses back at J Bar, so we should gripe?"

"Our saddles burned along with our rifles," guessed Stretch.

"We got cash enough to buy new ones," shrugged Larry.

"Counting your blessings, huh?" observed Tyne. "It's true what I've heard of you two. You take life one day at a time."

"Well . . . " Stretch grinned wearily. "We don't fret much. Frettin' makes a man old before his time, right runt?"

"Right," agreed Larry.

"How about him?" asked Tyne, gesturing to the unconscious Hartigan.

"I might take a look at him presently," said Larry. "Then again, I might leave him to Milt's hired hands. Gonna be a passel of 'em riding' in soon."

"Help is on the way?" prodded Tyne.

"We could make book on it," declared Larry. "I figure Milt's special stock ran all the way south to home range."

"Milt'll be plenty curious about that," Stretch predicted.

"The Ames gang probably hid their horses in that stand of timber," opined Tyne, staring westward. "I'd better make myself useful, ride over and take a look."

He was turning towards his horse when, from the north, he and the Texans heard the approaching vehicle. They watched as the buggy began the crossing of Clear Creek, Damien Blackwood driving with practiced ease, the fashionably-gowned Inez sharing the seat with him, at least until they were half-way across.

By coincidence, the kind that could only occur while Inez was around, a buggy wheel bumped the same submerged rock that had caused Mildred to stumble in that memorable first fording. The buggy lurched. The driver kept his seat, but Inez didn't.

"Clumsy, clumsy," sighed Stretch as, with a flurry of petticoats, she bounded off the buggyseat to flop in the water.

"Who are they?" asked Tyne, as Damien stalled the vehicle.

"We don't know him — just her," said Stretch.

They observed that Damien did what had to be done without leaving the seat. He bent over and down, grasped the wrist of a raised hand and, with no apparent difficulty, helped his companion reboard the vehicle.

"Friend of yours?" frowned Tyne.

"She comes by now and then," Larry said deadpan, "to fall in the creek."

"Nice lady," said Stretch. "Likes to visit and cook for us, but mostly she . . ."

"Falls in the creek," repeated Larry.

"Ain't that the truth," agreed Stretch.

"That doesn't make sense," protested Tyne.

"You're damn right," nodded Larry. "But it's what she always does."

Completing the crossing, Damien drove on almost all the way to the smoldering ruins of the line shack. When he stalled the buggy horse, he glanced briefly at the sprawled bodies and told Inez firmly,

"This isn't for your eyes — and you have to get out of those wet clothes anyway." He reached behind the seat for a rug. "Take this, go back to the creek, undress, wrap yourself in the rug and hang your clothes anywhere you can. Stay away from here till everything is dry."

"That could take hours," she complained. "Mister Lawrence, Mister Woodville, this is so embarrassing . . ."

"You've said that before," muttered Larry.

"Dear Lord, what could have *happened* here . . . ?" she fretted.

"Don't ask," growled Larry. "And don't linger. There's no shack for you to stoke up the stove and dry your duds. We don't even have rope for you to hang 'em on. Best do like your friend said. Take the rug, head on back to the creek and dry out."

"This is Damien Blackwood — I mentioned him," she murmured, as Damien helped her down.

The Texans acknowledged the introduction and identified Tyne, while Inez hurried back to the creek and the cashier soberly surveyed the scene of chaos.

"I get the impression," he remarked, "you gentlemen are lucky to be alive."

"We wouldn't be, if everything had gone right for these sonsabitches," Larry sourly assured him.

"A murder raid, Blackwood," said Tyne. "So, if your sympathy is aroused, it's better directed at Valentine and Emerson."

"Anything I can do to help?" Damien frowned at the Texans. They squatted side by side now, blackened and disheveled. "Your wounds . . ."

"Somebody at J Bar'll check us over,"

shrugged Larry. "Or send to Kimber for a doc."

Stretch explored his pockets and grimaced.

"Even our tobacco," he grouched to Larry.

"Cigars, gentlemen," offered Damien. "It seems so little at a time like this."

He produced four Long Nines. The Texans gratefully accepted, Larry assuring him,

"At a time like this, just what we need most."

The four lit up. Tyne worked his cigar to the side of his mouth, squinted toward the creek and recalled,

"I was about to go look for their horses. I'd better get on with it." He mounted the dun and started for the timber. Damien then hunkered in front of the Texans and asked,

"Does Inez know who you really are?"

"We told her Lawrence and Woodville, and that's no lie," said Larry.

"So there are only a handful of

us aware of your true identity and your reputation," said Damien. "Mister Jacklin no doubt, Mister Tyne, one of Sheriff Hallam's deputies — and me."

"These jaspers knew who they were gunnin' for," scowled Larry.

"Yes." Damien added sadly. "Almost succeeded, didn't they? If my sympathy irritates you, I apologize, but it's well meant, I assure you."

Their cigars were smoked down by the time Tyne returned, leading seven saddled horses. Larry counted the animals and frowned toward the rocks.

"Right," nodded Tyne. "Another body to be collected. Better leave it to me." He dismounted, walked to the rocks, found the seventh man and draped him over his shoulders. Toting his burden back to the ruins, he hung it across a horse. "Roy Joad," he announced. "His brother Noah is one of the other casualties. Ames wasn't the only killer of this bunch, Valentine. The Joad boys specialized in robbing and gunwhipping storekeepers. They had three murders to answer for."

"Was vengeance the motive for this attempt on your lives?" Damien asked the Texans.

"You got it, mister," sighed Stretch.

"All of 'em kin or friends of owlhoots we've tangled with," muttered Larry.

"Got a suggestion for you, Blackwood," said Tyne.

"Thanks, it already occurred to me," said Damien. "I should take Inez back to town as quickly as possible." He studied the sky. "A lot of cloud up there, not enough sun to dry her clothes. Won't be very dignified for her, I fear, but the rug will keep the cold out and the sooner she's indoors the better her chances of escaping a chill." About to leave them, he asked, "Should I advise the sheriff?"

"Sure, but no sense him comin' all the way out here," said Larry. "Milt'll have his boys take these stiffs to town and, if the sheriff got questions for my partner and me, he'll find us at J Bar."

A short time later, the bank cashier and his bedraggled passenger were en route to the county seat, the sodden garments bundled behind the seat, she wrapped in the rug with a third wrecked bonnet perched askew on her now-dry but disheveled head. During that journey, she pressed Damien for details of the attempt on the Texans' lives. All he told her was that their wounds weren't critical. They would survive.

The J Bar party arrived to find the stranger had been busy. All the losers, including the still-unconscious Hartigan, had been secured to their horses. Tyne stood by while the Texans recounted to Milt and the foreman all that had happened here, the attack, the firing of the shack, the stampede and the release of the cow-ponies, and the means by which they had escaped a fiery death.

"Nothin' left, Milt, 'cept what's in the cellar," Larry said dolefully. "We're sorry, but what else could we do but try to hold out against 'em?"

"*You're* sorry?" frowned Milt. "Hell, dumpin' you boys out here all by yourselves was *my* idea. I ought to be beggin' *your* pardon, doggone it."

"Shack can be rebuilt," Corrie said gruffly. "Always gonna have to be a line shack here."

"Better a new shack than two dead men — good men," insisted Milt. "And, listen boys, everything you lost, your rifles, spare duds, any other gear, J Bar'll replace it. On me, Larry. That's only fair."

"Figured you'd say that," nodded Larry. "Sorry about your prime herd."

"We didn't lose any, didn't find any carcasses on our way here," said Corrie. "Whole bunch made it safe to home range."

"We feel like we let you down, Milty," Stretch said contritely.

"Hogwash," snorted Milt.

"We ain't hurt so bad we couldn't tend 'em," offered Stretch.

"Yeh, sure," yawned Larry. "We

wouldn't mind campin' here if you want 'em driven back to this good graze."

"Winter's near over," muttered Milt. "They'll do good enough in my south quarter. And you boys're on the payroll for as long as you want to stay."

"Said we'd stay on till round-up's over," replied Larry. "We'll hold to that, Milt. But — uh . . ."

"Yup," nodded Milt. "You'll need to rest up a while 'fore you take on any chores." He nodded cordially to Tyne. "Guess you'll be headed for town with my hands. They'll be deliverin' these stiffs and turnin' the live one over to George Hallam."

"I should talk to the sheriff," said Tyne.

"The way Larry tells it, you showed up right when you were needed most," said Milt.

"My pleasure," said Tyne. "I mean that. You'll never know how much."

To Damien Blackwood's amusement, heads turned, eyes popped and townfolk converged on the Courier office when he stalled the buggy out front. Predictably, Inez was the centre of attention, hefting her bundle, struggling to keep her only covering tight about her, blushing furiously. Not only her aunt came to the doorway. So did both her uncles. Clara gave vent to a shocked gasp. Damien, loud enough for all to hear, assured her.

"It's not as bad as it looks. I can explain everything."

"It wouldn't *want* to be as bad as it looks," retorted Kinstry. "And it's mighty fortunate *somebody* can explain everything. Inside, you two."

"She's carrying her petticoats — and everything else," he heard one gaping woman remark to another. "Land's sakes! She must be naked under that rug!"

Striving to suppress his mirth, Damien conducted Inez across the threshold in courtly fashion. The Kinstrys followed them in, the editor awkward on his crutches, his brother closing the street-door and, on an afterthought, locking it and drawing the shades of the front windows. Damien then proceeded to account for Inez's unconventional appearance, she joining in, while the busybodies loitered out front, better than a double dozen of them now.

When all had been said, Kinstry assumed a stern demeanor and seized the best opportunity that had so far presented itself.

"Now Inez, we've never doubted your moral character," he pointed out. "And you know how we feel about Damien, a gentleman to the core. On the other hand, there's still the question of your reputation."

"Seems like every blabbermouth in Kimber City saw you in that get-up," remarked Eric. "There'll be a lot of talk."

"It would be better if . . . " began Clara.

"You took the words out of my mouth," nodded Kinstry. "The time has come, Inez."

"I agree, sir," drawled Damien. "This is the ideal time."

"You mean . . . ?" frowned Inez.

"You know damn well what we mean," growled Kinstry.

"Oh, well." She heaved a sigh and shrugged resignedly.

A few moments later, Eric unlocked and opened the street-door and Kinstry came out to face the crowd. Crowd was the word. People were packed tight all the way to the opposite sidewalk and one of Hallam's deputies trying to disperse them. Balancing on his crutches, the founder-editor of the Courier announced that his beloved niece was now betrothed to Mr Damien Blackwood and that the wedding date would be published in his next edition. There were approving smiles and warm applause, after which the gathering broke up.

The second sensation occurred an hour later, a party of J Bar riders led by Brad Tyne entering Main Street and proceeding to the office of the county sheriff, the tag riders leading seven laden horses by tie-lines. Hartigan was installed in a cell and a doctor summoned. Tyne then accompanied the bodies and Sheriff Hallam to the funeral parlor to assist in the identifications and answer the astonished lawman's many questions.

By mid-afternoon, Hallam was at J Bar to interrogate the victors of the battle of Clear Creek, who did their talking from horizontal positions in Bunkhouse Number 2 and accorded the boss-lawman all due courtesy. Hallam couldn't find fault, couldn't challenge their right to defend themselves. Even so, he was disgruntled.

"I'm wondering if I'll ever live it down," he complained. "The way it adds up, only Milt Jacklin and one of my deputies identified you. You tearaways have a reputation stretching from the east coast to the west and from North Montana to the Rio Grande — and I didn't know you were in my bailiwick, damn it."

"Tyne still around?" asked Larry.

"On his way home to Utah already,"

said Hallam, rising to leave.

"Gonna be a deputy again," guessed Stretch.

"I asked him — he said no," shrugged Hallam. "Said he has a job being held for him and a good woman waiting, said he plans on getting married."

Inez Durley presented her finished manuscript for her uncle's approval the week before she was to become Mrs Damien Blackwood. Having read every word of it, Kinstry mercilessly advised her,

"Forget it. No publisher would be interested — would even believe it. A searching analysis of the character of the West's most shiftless nomads you call it? Damn it, girl, your prose is too flowery. It gushes the way *you* gush when you talk of those drifters." He quoted passages. "'The grimly resolute and poignantly disturbed countenance of Lawrence Valentine — a disillusioned knight errant — his psyche deeply scarred, even more so than his Herculean body.'

Balderdash! Would you expect me to believe Valentine stripped naked to allow you to inspect his battle-scars? And this drivel about Emerson. 'More boy than man, shy, pitifully self-conscious in the presence of a woman trained in the arts of observation and analysis, a warrior, yea, but a warrior without guile, so towering of stature, so courageous in time of conflict, yet so lacking in maturity, so sweet of disposition, so gentle ... ' Confound it, could any publisher in his right mind stomach such nonsense? I strongly doubt it."

"You're shattering me," she complained.

"Damien'll pick up the pieces," he retorted, working up a paternal grin. "You two are a perfect match, so be thankful. You're what you are. He's a gentleman and he has a lot of patience — and by Godfrey he'll *need* it."

After spring round-up, their health and strength restored, the Texans were bade a fond farewell by Milt Jacklin and his womenfolk. Sitting new but well broken in saddles, new Winchesters housed in new saddle scabbards, toting ample provisions packed for them by the chuck-boss, mounted on their own animals, they rode north from the ranch headquarters. Montana, Larry had remarked, would not be too cold this time of year.

They paused only once before crossing Kimber County's north border. In sight of the scene of their most recent clash with the lawless, they reined up to roll cigarettes and study it all again, J Bar's best patch of graze, the brush to the east, the timber to the west, the cheerful creek and the hills to the north. On the site of the gutted line shack, a team of workmen were hard at it. A new shack was being built over the root cellar in which they had taken refuge. All that remained of what had once been their haven was the pile of charred wood carried clear of the building site and dumped by the workmen. They studied that black heap soberly. Stretch winced, heaved a sigh and remarked,

"Not this time, huh?"

"Not this time," nodded Larry.

"Rough while it lasted," recalled Stretch.

"The hell of it is, it could all happen again," grouched Larry. "No matter how far we drift or how safe we feel."

"We thought this was the safest place — plumb peaceful," muttered Stretch. "So now, I guess we just keep lookin', huh?"

"Uh huh," grunted Larry. "Just like always."

They rode on to ford the creek.

Books by Marshall Grover in the Linford Western Library:

BANDIT BAIT
EMERSON'S HIDEOUT
HEROES AND HELLERS
GHOST-WOMAN OF CASTILLO
THE DEVIL'S DOZEN
HELL IN HIGH COUNTRY
TEN FAST HORSES
SAVE A BULLET FOR KEEHOE
DANGER RODE DRAG
THE KILLER WORE BLACK
REUNION IN SAN JOSE
CORMACK CAME BACK
RESCUE PARTY
KINCAID'S LAST RIDE
7 FOR BANNER PASS
THE HELLION BREED
THE TRUTH ABOUT SNAKE RIDGE
DEVIL'S DINERO
HARTIGAN
SHOTGUN SHARKEY
THE LOGANTOWN LOOTERS
THE SEVENTH GUILTY MAN
BULLET FOR A WIDOW

CALABOOSE EXPRESS
WHISKEY GULCH
THE ALIBI TRAIL
SIX GUILTY MEN
FORT DILLON
IN PURSUIT OF QUINCEY BUDD
HAMMER'S HORDE
TWO GUNMEN FROM TEXAS
HARRIGAN'S STAR
TURN THE KEY ON EMERSON
ROUGH ROUTE TO RODD COUNTY

Other titles in the Linford Western Library:

TOP HAND
Wade Everett

The Broken T was big. But no ranch is big enough to let a man hide from himself.

GUN WOLVES OF LOBO BASIN
Lee Floren

The Feud was a blood debt. When Smoke Talbot found the outlaws who gunned down his folks he aimed to nail their hide to the barn door.

SHOTGUN SHARKEY
Marshall Grover

The westbound coach carrying the indomitable Larry and Stretch headed for a shooting showdown.